ISMAT CHUGHTAI was born in 1915 in Badayun and is counted among the earliest and foremost women Urdu writers. She focused on women's issues with a directness and intensity unparalleled in Urdu literature among writers of her generation. She is the author of several collections of short stories, novellas, a novel, *Terhi Lakir* (The Crooked Line), a collection of reminiscences and essays, *My Friend, My Enemy*, and a memoir, *Kaghazi Hai Perahan* (The Paper-thin Garment). With her husband, Shahid Latif, a film director, she produced and co-directed six films, and produced a further six, independently, after his death.

TAHIRA NAQVI, a translator of Urdu fiction and prose, taught English for twenty years, has taught Urdu at Columbia, and now heads the Urdu programme at New York University. She has translated Ismat Chughtai's short stories, her novel and her essays. She has also translated the works of Khadija Mastur, Sa'dat Hasan Manto and Munshi Premchand. Naqvi also writes fiction in English. She has published two collections of short fiction, *Attar of Roses and Other Stories of Pakistan* and *Dying in a Strange Country*. Her short stories have been widely anthologized.

MASOOMA

ISMAT CHUGHTAI

Translated from Urdu by Tahira Naqvi

SPEAKING
TIGER

SPEAKING TIGER PUBLISHING PVT. LTD
4281/4 Ansari Road, Daryaganj,
New Delhi—110002, India

WOMEN UNLIMITED
(an associate of Kali for Women)
7/10, Sarvapriya Vihar, First Floor
New Delhi – 110016, India

First published in India by Women Unlimited, an associate of
Kali for Women, 2011
This edition jointly published in paperback by Speaking Tiger and
Women Unlimited 2018

ISBN: 978-93-88070-81-2
eISBN: 978-93-88070-82-9

10 9 8 7 6 5 4 3 2 1

Printed at: Gopsons Papers Ltd

four months rent –
servants' salaries – amount owed to the shopkeeper –
electricity bill – washerman's bill –
children's school fees – water rises above my head –
drowning, I float up and see –
my living, breathing sixteen-year-old daughter –
skipping rope with her young friends

Ismat Chughtai

ONE

YES, THIS IS CHURCHGATE IN Bombay. No, there is no church near here to speak of, but there are many gates. If you get off the train and keep walking in a straight line, you will go past the weighing machine and cross the ice stand. On your left you will see the turnstiles used for exiting from the station. These barriers are for ticketless passengers who sneak in with the wave of women and children. Go through these turnstiles carefully, otherwise you will receive a sharp whack on your kneecap, which will leave you limping for days. Here you will observe two weary-looking ticket collectors, on either side of the turnstile, both deep in conversation. You may, if you wish, hand them an old ticket or even a stub from the weighing machine and pass through quickly and they will continue to chat, taking no notice of you. Arre bhai, watch your step! Right under the staircase runs a thin trickle of muck mixed with paan-juice spit. You can search all you want, but you won't be able to locate the source of this muck. Does it drop from the sky or spring from the earth? You will see nothing else like it. On the right, seated facing the wall, you'll observe a woman with a face like a plucked chicken. When there's light available from the sun or the lamppost, she carefully searches through her thinning, stringy hair extracting lice and fleas. She scrutinises these closely, a victorious smile spreading over her deeply-lined face, as if she's a diver who has risked life and limb to retrieve a pearl from the depths of the ocean. Then she places that wretched flea on her left thumbnail and proceeds to kill it with her right thumbnail. She does this as artfully as setting a rare gem on a delicate ring. She looks pleased as if she has finished off a fat-bellied usurer and the fire of vengeance blazing in her eyes momentarily cools. When a pile of corpses accumulates on her nail, she rubs her nail on the wall to clean it off and then sends her fingers in search of new prey. Be mindful of her rags and other belongings as you go past her, or else she'll stare at you as if you've forced your way into the bedroom of a young woman in seclusion!

Just look out for the cars going in both directions as you step over onto the footpath and don't hit the barber's elbow with your knee, brother, or else his hand may slip and make a gash on the head of his customer. This woman selling rotten bananas is the owner of the paan and bidi basket. Jump over it carefully – well done!

As you reach Satkar Hotel, protect your nose from the odour of stale idlis, cross the mysterious patch of sludge, and jump over the bhelpuri-wallah's bucket. That's perfect! Now, avoiding the assault of legs belonging to filmstar Neelam's adopted children perched on the wall, and artfully dodging the gravel pile, keep going straight until you run into A.R. Malik's box-like shop. It's all right – this is A Road, you'll always find a few bumps and potholes here. Just ignore everything and keep going, slipping and sliding over banana peels and getting entangled in dog leashes. Now stop!

Across from Jaiband College, the building enclosed by the

boundary wall on which you'll see the greatest number of kids perched together, is Indus Court. Sitting on one section of the wall, next to the central gate, are young adolescent girls and on the other side are young boys looking awkward and gawky. In the demeanour of the girls you will catch glimpses of Marilyn Monroe, Brigitte Bardot and Sandra Dee, and in the boys you will see reflections of Elvis Presley, Jimmy Dean and Ricky Nelson. This wall is of great importance to the inhabitants of Indus Court – this is where romances materialise, engagements take place, and marriages are planned, resulting in gems that can be studded onto this wall. Oblivious of this cyclical process, the wall remains a silent victim of paan-juice sprays and the posters of vote-seekers.

On the ground floor of Indus Court is Guru Granthji's shrine. Dressed in a grimy dhoti and undershirt, a fat-bellied priest with a youthful face can usually be seen standing on the stairs, yawning. The lemon-sized knot of hair on his bald scalp is always soaked in oil. Actually, rock'n'roll film music is played here all day long. At night a great deal of frankincense is burned and hymns are sung. The priest gets bored with singing regular hymns and so makes up tunes based on film music, and beats his drum late into the night.

And when one hears "*red, red cheeks*", and "*silk shalwar*", one becomes convinced of the nature of God's power to bestow blessings. His grace is unique. If He wishes He can make flowers bloom from stone and make rock'n'roll ring out of mosques and temples!

The first among the string of flats is my house.

If you stand on the balcony facing the qibla and make a forty-degree turn, you have a clear view of Nilofar's flat. Yes, the same one that's the most showy-looking of all the flats, the one in which the walls are painted a dark turquoise and pink, and where silk curtains shimmer in the brightness of neon lights. Yes, the same building in front of which these big, expensive cars are parked. These cars arrive here early in the evening and depart in the morning after the all-night celebration. Their drivers consort with the ayahs in the nearby building while their owners conduct the business of pleasure in the glimmering flat in the front. Close at hand is the place for procuring smuggled liquor.

That beauty with a soft and supple body is the one who runs the show in this flat. I've put you through all this trouble and given you all this detailed information just to bring you to this very flat so that you won't veer off to the place where hymns are sung to the tunes of film songs. When Nilofar was born, the Quran had been consulted to find the name "Masooma Bano" for her. A daughter after three sons – she had been thoroughly pampered. At her birth her aunt and uncle, Khala jani and Bade Mamu had had a fight; they had both wanted her to be engaged to their respective sons. Two sisters, Zubaida and Haleema came after her and by the time the last child, a boy, was about a year old, all hell had broken loose.

In Hyderabad, the land graced by God, plans were being made under Qasim Rizvi's command to fly flags at the Red Fort in Delhi. Majid, the father of Masooma, alias Nilofar, was a special member of this army and the moment the alarm went off he took flight, taking with him his older sons, all his savings, all the expensive jewellery, and the papers for the houses.

The baby and the three girls were left with the wife. The plan was that they would all be sent for once he had settled down. But no one knows what happened after he got there, as they were never sent for. The older sons got married, secured well-paid jobs, and were allotted houses and land, but they did not think about their mother, sisters and younger brother.

Whatever the husband had left behind sustained them

for some time, then she tried to pay for their living expenses by selling the little jewellery that remained. For a few days the bracelets were chewed, then the *jugnu*, *champakali* and *naugharian* were gobbled up. Finally the armlet and the girls' jewellery also descended into the stomach's hoarding sack. Who can know all the details? But something must have happened to make her finally pack up and come to Bombay.

People are of the opinion that she came to Bombay because one can get a good price for everything here. Bombay is the city of adoring admirers, where enthusiastic patrons pay generously. Whether it's old cars or jewellery belonging to the mistresses of noblemen, sons capable of procuring jobs, or attractive daughters – all fetch a higher price in Bombay. For a while the Begum stayed with an acquaintance, but when she began to reveal her imperious nature, he got her a flat in Dadar as a favour. The poor man paid part of the rent, the rest he borrowed. He never demanded anything in return for any of these favours. All Ehsaan sahib did was come by early in the evening, play with the kids, chat and then leave around twelve or one. The Begum had thrived on a diet of pure ghee, but a few grey hairs were now beginning to show. She wanted marriage and insisted on a nikah, but the sympathetic friend failed to show up for eight days on the pretext that he had to take care of something important. When she saw his face on the ninth day, her eyes brimmed with tears.

Two years passed. Saleem's school expenses and the girls' needs continued to be met with difficulty. Some brass utensils had been left behind in Hyderabad, and the Begum decided to dispose these off. She was gone for a week.

On her return she found the children as she had left them, but for some reason she felt that Masooma had suddenly matured. Anxiety about her marriage descended into her heart like a dagger. When Masooma came out after her bath, drying her hair and dressed in a flowered housecoat, the Begum was taken aback. This expensive new towel, this flowered housecoat – these had not been there before!

And then the storm broke. If she had her way the Begum would grind Masooma into mincemeat and throw her to the dogs, but Masooma swore vehemently that Ehsaan sahib had taken her out, helped her shop for lipstick and powder, bought her a dressing gown, but that nothing else had happened. The Begum's tears had dried up a long time ago. All night she tossed and turned, heaving long sighs.

When Ehsaan sahib arrived the following day, she was furious. Her manner pricked him like a stiff thorn embedded in his side.

"You're upset for no reason," he protested. "They're like my daughters. What is so awful about my buying them something? Don't I buy things for Amina, for Farida?"

"But is Masooma your only darling daughter? Are Zubaida and Haleema only your stepdaughters? And Saleem a mere charity case! This bitch gets everything?"

"Look, you're always giving me a hard time. How can one have a conversation with you? Actually, Ahmad bhai, my friend, you know, he was the one who bought the things – he owns a general store. Saleem also picked out a hockey stick and a Meccano set."

"Who is this Ahmad bhai?"

"He's a general merchant, he lives in Bandra, he's a millionaire – he has a shop in the market, and another one in Colaba. He also has a furniture shop in Bandra. He's a very important man."

The Begum looked at him incredulously.

"Really, and you didn't mention a thing. I didn't have the nerve to say anything to you earlier – after all, you're the guardian of my girls – but if some arrangement can be made – although I don't have anything to give them."

"Yes, yes, don't worry about any of that." He looked a little embarrassed. "He has also just bought a flat in Dadar – paid cash for it."

A wave of gratitude gushed from the Begum's heart. Finally the kids went to bed. She stayed up, and sitting down next to Ehsaan sahib, made paans for him, popping them into his mouth with her own hand.

"So why don't you bring Ahmad bhai over one day."

"He came several times in your absence. You know, I thought it best not to let this opportunity go."

"Well, you're the one in charge here. But do invite him for dinner tomorrow."

Ahmad Bhai Suratwallah arrived the following day. About forty-five years old, he was dressed in a drab-looking pyjama topped by a dark brown achkan, and wore a Rumi cap on his head. The Begum was rendered speechless when she saw him. She thought: *this fellow wouldn't have looked so ludicrous if he had dyed his hair instead of colouring it with henna.*

He had brought a necklace with him, which he presented to Masooma.

"Oooh, I don't want it," Masooma said coyly.

"Why not?" Ahmad bhai leered, his paan-covered teeth exposed in a smile.

"I just don't like it."

"If you don't like this one, I'll bring you another one."

"I won't take that either." Masooma broke into a spirited laugh and ran out of the room. Her coquettish behaviour overpowered Ahmad bhai's senses.

"Is it possible to take the girl out today?" he asked. "Can you get permission, please?" he whispered in Ehsaan sahib's ear.

"Look here, keep your eyes to yourself for now, all right? Otherwise everything will be ruined."

"If the wretch wants more money, that's no problem – I'll pay," Ahmad bhai pleaded.

"No, no, it's not a question of money. She's a girl from a good family. She's just turned sixteen. No one has yet glimpsed even the hem of her dupatta. Such impatience won't do here. Haste is the devil's work." Ehsaan sahib tried to make him understand the situation.

But when the Begum realised that he was playing the pimp, her eyes blazed in anger.

"Look at the face of that shabby, dishevelled fool. Is this worm-eaten kebab the only person left for my dainty daughter? He'll blacken his face if he marries such a young girl."

In a very gentle voice, Ehsaan sahib explained that Ahmad bhai was not so despicable as to think of carrying out a nikah with the girl. And in any case he couldn't do it. His father-in-law was an influential man – he wouldn't leave a single hair on his balding head if he took a second wife.

The Begum was transformed into a firecracker at this news. Sparks flew in all directions. Her only kindness was to refrain from giving Ehsaan sahib a thorough thrashing.

Ahmad bhai became despondent when he was given the news!

"You must think I'm an idiot – first you say the girl is available, then you say she's not – what is this nonsense?"

"It's a job that can't be rushed, seth. How long can ripe fruit stay on the branch? Trust me. You won't find high quality goods lying on the footpath. Be patient and wait a few more days."

"All right, I'll be patient – but how many days?" Ahmad bhai drew a long sigh like a real lover.

"Rita is about to deliver, seth, and she will make trouble. Wait until the situation with her has cooled off."

"What are you saying? I pay all the expenses for that wretch Rita, and I'll keep paying. Why are you worrying? She won't be any trouble. I've talked to Pir bhai. He has already received an advance on the flat from me."

"Are you selling the Santa Cruz flat?"

"What can I do if I don't sell? My father-in-law is giving me a hard time. That wretched girl is of low morals, he says."

"Which girl?" Making sense of what Ahmad bhai said was no laughing matter.

The truth of the matter was that he was tired of Rita. She was always whining. He had been complaining for a while that even his wife didn't smoulder with jealousy the way Rita did. She had sent spies out after him. Pir bhai had been an admirer of hers for a long time. The relationship had progressed and Ahmad bhai had finally handed over the house with everything in it along with Rita to Pir bhai. Now she was pregnant and neither man wanted to take the responsibility for her condition. A man whom Rita had passed off as her brother used to visit her often. It was later discovered that he was an ex-fiancé. He had been absent for six years and when he returned he was up to his old tricks again – the child she was expecting was his. Ahmad bhai had not visited her for many months. Suddenly he no longer fancied her – the sight of her face made him feel sick. Pir bhai may look shabby, but he owned a great deal of property. His wife had died. He was even willing to marry Rita, but she was vacillating. If she married him then the poor fellow would have to find another mistress, she thought.

"Even so seth," Ehsaan sahib said, "you can't easily find another girl like Masooma. Trust me. I've started tightening the chains. Your work will be done soon."

But Ahmad bhai continued to despair.

"That rascal Roopchandji's film assistant, Lallji, introduces him to so many girls. These social film-wallahs are no good. Roopchandji said to me: 'Come with me, we're going to Lok Khandala to check out a location with a bunch of girls.' He asked me to bring two cases of beer and whisky. I said, 'Bhai, first I'll see what I get, then next week I'll send the case of whisky.' What a lively bunch of girls!" Ahmad bhai mixed the girls up with the bottles.

"Roopchandji is a crook. Lallji was protesting that he had been swindled by him. He keeps writing IOUs but never makes a payment. The set has been standing for seven days and the second heroine is nowhere to be seen. If you complain, he says get another one. Now imagine, how can you get another girl in the middle of the picture?"

"You'll have to get another one," Ahmad bhai laughed.

The second heroine thought she was about to be married to Roopchandji, but Ehsaan sahib knew that he wasn't going to get married again.

Once he had mollified Ahmad bhai, albeit with some difficulty, Ehsaan sahib came up with a new plan for tightening the screws on the Begum and began implementing it with force.

Sunk in mire up to her waist, the Begum was trying to save herself. But the slightest movement served only to pull her down deeper. The cobra's jaws were expanding. Six months of rent was overdue. The cook complained every day. The rogue managed to take out his share from even a tiny lump of salt. The meat he bought was nearly all skin and membranes. He picked vegetables from a pile of rubbish and charged her full price. In the market, it is customary for traders to heap piles of rotting vegetables in baskets which are then either sold to hotels or to poor people at low rates. Sometimes one can find chunks of fresh vegetables mixed up with rotting pieces in these piles.

The Begum knew that the cook managed to recover his wages in this way, but she didn't have the courage to scold him. The only person he was scared of was Ehsaan sahib, but these days he had became quiet and restrained and the cook had become more audacious. The girls had been complaining that he was peeping at them whenever he had a chance. The glass panes on the doors had been painted over with white varnish; in a couple of places someone had scratched off enough paint to make a peephole and frequently when the girls were changing, these scratched areas would suddenly be filled with black shadows.

The children's school fees had not been paid and threats that their names would be struck from the register were pouring in. The doctor's bills had not been settled in a year. Ehsaan sahib was the one who had opened an account in the Begum's name, but he had no idea that the bills had been gradually mounting. As for the milk-seller, he finally confronted him and demanded payment.

Ehsaan sahib became exasperated. "I don't have Qaroon's treasure in my possession – I too have a family to think of, you know," he said helplessly.

But the Begum did not soften. Around this time someone proposed that she try to get her daughters into films – they would be successful as actresses, it was suggested. In those days there were several producers and directors living in Dadar and Shivaji Park. She met them all one by one, making unsuccessful trips to Ranjeet Studios and she also came with a friend of hers to see me. But we had already finished with the casting for our film. And the way she boasted about her superior lineage irritated me no end. It seemed as though she was not only doing a special favour to the film industry, but also to future generations of my family by introducing Masooma Bano to the film world. She was also under the misconception that a contract could be signed right away with an immediate advance. But for a whole week she couldn't even get to meet a producer. She waited in vain. No one would even look at her, let alone agree to meet her. After all, why would anyone notice shy and bashful Masooma, dressed in such plain clothes?

The Begum's haughtiness made matters worse. She displayed an air of self-importance whenever she met anyone.

Really, what could an amateur manageress do with a vivacious young girl like Masooma? So as expected, the debts kept mounting. The landlord began making more aggressive demands for the rent; the children's names were struck off from the school register; the soles of her shoes were worn out from endless trips to the studios – and still no one bothered to give Masooma a proper look. But the straw that broke the Begum's back was the news that her husband had taken a second wife. The old man had wed a nineteen-year-old wisp of a girl and had promised to send the Begum divorce papers.

That day she shut herself in her room and wept inconsolably. But then she got up, washed and braided her hair and gave the cook instructions to fetch Ehsaan sahib. When the cook tried to hum and haw, she yelled at him with such force that he immediately dashed off. The Begum had come a long way in just a few hours.

Ehsaan sahib arrived to find the Begum lying down with an arm flung across her forehead.

"Allah, what airs you put on now – I have to send special invitations to you. I'll have an invitation card printed and ready in case one needs to call you in future."

Ehsaan sahib drew a long breath and fell at her feet.

That day the Begum's family pride died. She conceded and laid out her terms. The flat would be in the girl's name. A thousand a month with no questions asked. The girl would not spend a night out without her permission. Perhaps this was her way of getting back at her husband – there he was grinding someone's nineteen-year-old, here a price was being settled for his daughter of the same age. When the old man found out his daughter was selling herself, he would be in for a rude awakening.

"Today? No, no – I need some more time." She exploded at Ehsaan's proposition.

"All this time you need has ruined my plans," he replied

irately. "That bastard, Ahmad bhai, is not even willing to provide signing money, he says he has no influence. How can you trust a man like that?"

When the surgeon extends the knife to excise the wound, the patient beseechingly grabs his hand. "Wait just a little, just a little ..." she said.

But the surgery has to be performed. How long can the surgeon wait?

"The girl is feeling a bit down," Ehsaan sahib tried to appease Ahmad bhai.

"Oh, let the girl be. I'm leaving for Poona today."

"And when will you be back?"

"I'll spend the racing season there. I've been thinking, the Navyug studio is for sale there. I'll buy it."

"No, no, forget Navyug. There's nothing left there. The minute you clean out the rubbish, half your money will be gone. And that crafty Mrs Mitchell is making a fool of you. All that the strumpet has is rotting goods. Worn out, degenerate Anglo-Indian girls, scraps left behind by the white man. And anyway you won't be able to put up with Seth Sajhe's merchandise."

Ahmad bhai was a born coward. He winced.

"What's the rush, seth? The girl will be ready by Saturday," Ehsaan winked.

"You're joking" Ahmad bhai broke into a smile.

"I swear on your head. All right, come on then, let's go and get the supplies at least – the film set will be ready by tomorrow."

These seths think that they have the monopoly on brains. They'll buy everything in person and go and look at all the materials themselves to ensure that the producer doesn't swindle them. But producers are also very clever – they insist they will not charge a single penny until the film does good business and until then will be satisfied with receiving only what has been spent on the production.

Timber for use on the set was purchased at the cost of twenty thousand rupees. First Ahmad bhai swindled himself: in other words he paid fifteen thousand rupees for the timber, but had a receipt made for twenty thousand. Then when Ehsaan sahib went to pick up the fifteen-thousand-rupee purchase, he had only ten thousand rupees worth of merchandise loaded; the rest he returned in exchange for four thousand rupees. The shopkeeper saved a thousand. This wood was transported to the studio and calculations were then made as to who needed how much. The wood for ten thousand rupees was surreptitiously disposed off for a total of twelve thousand and a small quantity retained for the set. When Ahmad bhai dropped in to make sure all was in order, a random set that had already gone into construction was shown to him. The carpenter readily went along with everything.

This sort of thing happened with costumes as well. Cash memos were collected from friends for garments and shown to the seth. These were also useful for income tax purposes. But if the seth was clever then a deal would be made with the shopkeeper. For fabric that actually cost three thousand he would prepare a bill for four thousand. Five hundred for him and five hundred for you. But some seths were very clever. They would insist that the cloth be purchased from their uncle's shop and stitched at their other uncle's shop, so that there was no room for unfair play. However, if the seth got into trouble and his money had been spent, then the cameraman would have to be recruited to have the order cancelled: "No, no, this won't do at all – it will rip," the cameraman would say and the seth would have no recourse. Although he was charging forty per cent interest, he wanted all the money coming in to be seen as his profit. He wanted to tack on all his expenses to film profits: employees' salaries, children's expenses, the rent for his house deducted as an office expense, recreational expenses, and all those incurred in the love and devotion offered to his mistresses.

In the meantime the producer was also telling himself that what he could get now may not be available later. The distributor showed no profits in any other films except those that were super hits. It was obvious what kind of a film it would turn out to be when there were so many vultures circling over it. It would be released and would flop in its first week, the producer and financier flopping along with it.

After hours of aggravating debate, Ahmad bhai finally softened. It was decided that as soon as he had recorded two songs, Masooma would be his.

These two songs were being recorded on credit. Pleas and entreaties directed to Asha Bhosle made her finally agree to the job, but with the understanding that payment would come from the Bombay territory. The studio and raw materials had been acquired at an interest of three per cent. The musicians were ready to work on credit as well. And so at long last the songs were recorded.

All night the Begum paced restlessly on the balcony. She had agreed, but how was she going to do it? Was she going to bluntly broach the subject with Masooma? She couldn't do it. There were moments when she wanted to wake her up, clasp her to her bosom, and explain. But explain what? All her life she had told the girl: "Dear daughter, a woman's jewels are her honour. Lose your life but don't let your honour be tarnished." How could she now say to her, "We have no one left who can support us except you, you'll have to make this sacrifice, you'll have to be the oar that will propel the boat that is carrying your younger brother and sisters."

No, she couldn't say this. She wept into the morning hours. In the distance the gates of the Krishna Mill were opening to let out tired labourers who had worked all night and were now walking wearily, looking like sugarcane stalks that had been squeezed dry. The next shift of groups of fresh-looking men, young and old, with their dhotis tightly folded between their thighs, and women laughing merrily, were all making their way in through the gates. In the bright morning light, scraps of paper used for wrapping snacks and leaves strewn about showed up on the black surface of the road like marks on a leper's face. A scrawny, emaciated dog stood next to a lamppost, leg lifted, urinating.

She returned to her room. Suddenly her gaze was riveted on Masooma's sleeping form: how soundly she slept. Her face was partially hidden by a jumble of tousled hair, two teeth shimmered through half-open pink lips and the edges of her shirt, tucked under her body, had pushed up the neckline. The Begum leaned over and opened the top buttons of the shirt – one, two, three – there lay an innocent, youthful, white bosom, quivering with the heartbeat of passionate dreams!

Resting against the bed, she wept uncontrollably until the impatient Bombay sun peeped through the window. The rag hanging in the window stirred and all at once it seemed as if a coiled snake was poised over a milk container, waiting to swoop down. Shaken, she hastily covered up the girl with the blanket.

TWO

WHAT CELEBRATIONS. A DAUGHTER had been born after three sons, delicate in build. She was like that even in her mother's belly; one could tell since in the case of a boy the mother's belly would push up against her breasts. Masooma was as small as a bird, her presence in the womb hardly felt by the mother. As a baby she would be satisfied with just a tiny amount of milk and the mother had too much milk. It is said that if a mother has a lot of milk the child is very lucky and wealth follows. The astrologer had taken one look at her forehead and said: "She's a very lucky child, she'll bring much prosperity in her wake, there will be an elephant in attendance at her door."

Elephant indeed! Ahmad bhai was no more than a donkey!

The girl had indeed brought good luck: that same year her father had been promoted. She was a year old when he was awarded a title, received the command of a battalion and was showered with favours by the government.

She began her periods in her thirteenth year and proposals began raining down on the parents. Proposals from rich and eminent nawabs. "Unh! These nawabs are good for nothing. We'll marry her to an ICS officer."

The mother had thought: *for her wedding I'll have a drummer playing the dhol a week before the festivities start. The wedding will be conducted exactly in the tradition of old weddings. She'll be secluded for nine days to observe the manjha ceremony. For her body rub we will use Delhi's ubtan paste that is well known. The mehndi will be prepared from the leaves of the bushes at home.*

Her paternal grandfather had planted a cutting for his granddaughter's wedding. By now it had spread underneath the entire veranda. At every Eid, when young girls came looking to pluck the henna leaves, they were shooed off; they might shake the bush to its roots, it was feared. It was hoped that the mehndi bush would outlast the granddaughter's wedding.

But then came the police action and there was little else anyone could think about. Her husband had left. All the bushes dried up. The bungalow had remained vacant. Even the foundations were eaten away by termites. When the Begum went back there to collect her possessions she saw that where once the mehndi bush had bloomed, now the foundations of a bathroom were being laid down. The dried up mehndi bush lay atop a pile of rubbish. Its desiccated leaves crumbled at the touch of her hand. Her heart stopped for a minute. The mehndi plant withering away like this was not a propitious omen. She had planned to prepare seven kinds of dishes at her daughter's wedding. *Pulao, qorma, tandoori, stuffed chicken, shahi tukre, seekh kebab – and ...* the aroma of these foods wafted into her nose as she thought about them now.

Everyone had tea and toast that evening. Ehsaan sahib was not willing to spend even a penny until he had received the goods. But the Iranian restaurant owner was still being gracious and the loan with interest was sure to be paid back one day. When ripe fruit hangs from the branches of a tree, the people in the vicinity do not hesitate to bring their pots to water the roots.

How long could the she-goat keep her young ones safe? The day arrived. As had been planned, the two younger girls were dispatched late in the afternoon to Ehsaan sahib's house to spend the night. Masooma had insisted on accompanying them but the Begum angrily shut her up. The entire incident was to appear as a coincidence. Masooma had not been asked to wear anything special, although according to custom, the sacrificial goat is garlanded once at least. When Ehsaan sahib appeared with Ahmad bhai in the evening, the Begum broke out in a sweat, as if it was her honour at stake, not her daughter's.

There was some small talk for a while.

"The industry's days are numbered. A producer was nearly killed by a bunch of extras the other day. The person in charge of costumes stole garments and sold them; he had been deprived of a year's pay. Now except for the hero and heroine, or their toadies, no one else can make it in films. It's these very people who are now going to take care of distribution also. Then a day will come when they'll also own the cinema halls."

"And then they'll be the ones watching films in the cinema halls," the Begum said, trying to keep the conversation going.

But Ahmad bhai was waiting impatiently for what he had come for. All this beating about the bush was making him cantankerous. He was very drunk, and yet he kept taking out a flask from his pocket and, turning his back to them, swigging from it. A copy of *True Story* in her hands, Masooma lay casually on her back, reading in the light of the dim bulb. Ahmad bhai was getting restless. He scratched his head, played with his moustache, and felt an odd titillation inside his thighs. The irises of his eyes were spinning. The Begum was stalling as if she expected the surgeon's scalpel to become blunt, or as if a potion for all her sorrows would suddenly start raining down from the sky. But for how long could she stall? She drew a heavy breath and rose to her feet. For a moment she felt like spitting in his face: "You bastard, you have unwed daughters too, go and take a look at them, the daughters for whom you've filled your almiras. Have you taken money out of these almiras and come to buy my Masooma with it? As if she too is a sack of flour, or a canister of ghee?" But the water had risen above her head. Drowning, she finally said:

"I'll be back in a minute. I have to get some papad from Lakshmibai next door." The cook had already been given the evening off. Masooma didn't suspect a thing and the Begum left.

"Look, I've got a date for a recording. I'll be back in an hour," Ehsaan sahib said, loudly enough for Masooma to hear. "Ahmad bhai, wait here, the girl is alone. You can leave when the Begum returns. Come to the studio later and listen to some dance music. How well Shamshad has performed this song. I swear, compared to this, Naushad's tune is nothing. It's a very exciting song. When the hero is injured in a car accident, the same tune is injected with sadness. Then in the dream sequence I'm having it adapted to a waltz, for a duet. And what's more, when the heroine's baby is ill, like a lullaby it ..."

"Yes, yes, I know all that," Ahmad bhai said impatiently. "Go now. What's the purpose of all this useless chattering?"

"All right, all right," Ehsaan sahib said, his spirits dampened.

Then suddenly it was as if there was no one in the house. No one in Bombay. No one in the world! The only ones left were the oblivious Masooma curled up in the murky light of the fly-infested bulb and the scabby Ahmad bhai.

Far away somewhere, someone kicked a wounded puppy,

which began yelping as it scampered into a gutter. Her head bent low, the Begum walked hurriedly towards the bus stop. Tears flowing from her eyes blurred her vision, making the path ahead look unfamiliar. In the darkness no one noticed her tears.

After getting off the bus a few stops away the Begum spent a long time buying things from the small shops. After that she walked around the Khuda Daad Circle a few times. Then she thought she would see a show at the Broadway Cinema. But she was suddenly overcome with a feeling of horror and retraced her steps. There were innumerable couples strolling about in Shivaji Park. Some distance away, in front of Cadel Court, a few hoodlums were singing the songs of the rainy season to the beat of a kettledrum. She continued walking till she reached the sandy beach and strolled on it for a while. Finally, sitting on the cool sand, she began weeping softly.

The ocean was sobbing before her, the water gently swelling. She wept ceaselessly. People strolled past talking in whispers. A silvery laugh would arise and then be drowned out by a heavy voice. She scooped up sand in both hands, squeezed her fists, and stifled her screams.

How alone she was. The world had forgotten her. How Nawab sahib had begged her father for her hand for his son, what hopes he'd had. Her husband had never spoken harshly to her, indeed he treated her like a delicate flower. How warm that love was! How hot youth was! A sweet drowsiness filled her eyes in those days but her husband was always intent on waking her up, begging her. And today, while Masooma's fate was being decided, he was probably fast asleep with a young bride clasped to his bosom.

A storm of rage burst in her heart. The bills in her purse began to hiss. To hell with the nikah! What's in a nikah? Her own nikah had been conducted by the Bade Qazi sahib, the one who had conducted innumerable nikahs for a rich old man. Today that nikah had become even more insignificant than these grains of sand.

People were slowly leaving. Two or three caretakers were loitering around her. All at once her heart beat convulsively. What was this foolishness? She was carrying five thousand rupees with her. Not one or two rupees, but a full five thousand. She dusted off the sand from her hands and started on her way back. When she reached home she saw that the entire building was plunged in darkness. Jumping over rows of naked legs on the footpath, she hastened her step.

She heard a muffled scream and then, rushing out of the darkness, Masooma grabbed her.

"Ammi! Ammijan, my Ammijan!" Trembling, she threw the weight of her body into her mother's arms. In the dim light of the stars she saw that Masooma's blouse was torn at the neck, her sari was in shreds, her hair was tangled up, her silken white neck had scratch marks, and blood had dripped from one earlobe and congealed as if she had been mauled by hungry dogs. Clasping her daughter to her breast, the mother withered. Forgot all her plans. She had thought she would scold her, call her depraved and debauched, so that she could maintain the image of her own respectability. Conceal her own crime. The incident would be seen as an accident. But she didn't remember any of this.

When she stepped inside the flat she was stunned. Masooma had made a clean escape and turned Ahmad bhai to pulp.

It seemed as if the entire place had been overrun by wild horses. The water jugs lay shattered, the glasses had rolled on the floor, the tea set was in smithereens, the clothes from the clothesline were scattered everywhere and the glass panes on the windows had been smashed.

Enraged, the Begum felt her blood boil. She slapped Masooma's face with force.

"You bitch!"

"But Ammi ... that wicked man ..." Masooma couldn't understand what was happening.

"Shut up, you wretch! May God help us, you've destroyed the house. Will your father pay for all this damage?" With both hands she clutched the bag with the money to her breast. "Oh God, why don't you send me death? Not one but four corpses weighing on my chest, and look at the way they act. Bitch, harlot ..." She cursed her daughter angrily. The mother who moments ago had clasped her daughter to her breast was now suddenly fearful of the rustling sound of rupee bills. The money would have to be returned tomorrow!

She refused to listen to Masooma's pleas as she squatted on the mat in her wet and tattered clothes, crying hysterically. Early next morning the Begum saw Ehsaan sahib and trembled like an animal being led to slaughter by a butcher. But he smiled affectionately and sat down beside her.

"I'm coming straight from seeing Ahmad bhai. What an idiot! I scolded the fool."

The Begum quietly took out the wad of bills from her purse and threw it in front of Ehsaan sahib.

"What's this?" he said gently and started counting the rupees. "Now, how can it be our fault? Ahmad bhai is a complete idiot. He had had too much to drink. I scolded him, the damn fool. We should be grateful our flat is at the back and the neighbours next door were away on a trip to Nasik. If anyone had realised what was going on the police would have been called and the wretch would have landed himself in jail." He fingered the money, then pushed it toward her. "No need to worry. She doesn't know anything yet, she'll come around eventually. You're the mother, you can explain and cajole her."

If the Begum had not been all choked up she would have asked, "What's there to explain?"

"By God, why are you crying? I've told the landlord and he'll be stopping by for the rent. Have some clothes made for the girl. Actually, here's what you should do. Go to the market. I have an account there with Moolchand."

So Ahmad bhai was not angry. In fact he was very much taken with the young girl's coquetry.

"I say, what a ferocious little thing she is," he had said to Ehsaan sahib, rubbing an ice cube on his swollen nose. His clothes were tattered as well, but despite that he couldn't stop smiling. "What a girl, just like a wild doe."

"But seth, was it decent to get so drunk and then torment the poor girl like this?"

Ahmad bhai began muttering excuses.

"I'll go slow today. But, I won't go back to that flat."

"It won't be today."

"Why not?"

"It just won't."

"What are you saying? You scoundrel, you take five thousand from me and ..."

"Put it on my account."

"On your account?"

"Yes. I'll get the money from Surajmal in a day or two and I'll give it all back to you. What do you think? That you're the only millionaire in all of Bombay?"

"What's this talk? When did I say you have to return the money?"

"Sethji, will you listen to me carefully?"

"Yes, what do you want to say?"

"This girl?"

"Yes?"

"She's not someone you can handle."

"Why not?"

"My word, what a nincompoop you are! This chit of a girl beat you to a pulp."

"No, no, it wasn't like that. I had been drinking that stuff neat. I couldn't see anything. And the girl, why she was so feisty, I can't tell you. I just touched her and she started hitting me."

"Well, think carefully."

"I've decided. Today, I'll take whatever happens."

"Look here, you are being stupid repeating the same thing, like a parrot. All right, here's what you do. You know Flory?"

"Don't talk to me about Flory. She's a third-rate girl. What do you take me for?"

"All right, all right, don't get all worked up."

"Why shouldn't I get worked up? I paid five thousand for Masooma. It's no small sum."

"Listen my friend, what do you want me to do? Shall I tie up her hands and feet and bring her to you?"

"No, no, of course not. But can't you talk to her? Tell her she shouldn't get so angry."

Ehsaan bhai became irritated and swore at him.

"Listen," Ahmad bhai said calmly, "do you want a dance by Cuckoo?"

"If I have a dance number by Cuckoo the film is sure to be a hit."

"All right then. Take the damn dance. Take two dance numbers."

The seth again bared his teeth in a smile.

"Hmm." Ehsaan sahib nonchalantly lit a cigarette.

But Ahmad bhai was obsessed with Masooma.

"All right, I'll have a talk today," Ehsaan sahib relented.

"You wretch! What's this 'I'll have a talk' business?" Ahmad bhai became incensed. "You're just a crook!"

"Look here seth! Don't say things that will get you a

thrashing." Ever since the seth had become besotted with Masooma, Ehsaan sahib had started acting quite boldly. He knew the seth was a fool and once he became obsessed with something he wouldn't give it up under any circumstances. "Ah, I just remembered. The bill from Maganlal dress-wallah is still pending."

"It doesn't matter. I'll give you a cheque tomorrow. I didn't say I wouldn't?"

"And call Moolchand."

"Moolchand? I gave him a cheque yesterday. Baba, you'll finish me off. I'll ..."

"Oh, what a fool I have to deal with! This is not for the picture. Begum was saying that the girls do not have nice clothes. I've also made arrangements in Dadar for a much larger flat for them."

"Oh, I see. Why didn't you say so before?" The seth snorted. "I'll send over a sari in the evening and I'll also call Moolchand. But it should be today ..."

"All right, all right."

The Begum picked up the bundle of rupees and realised it wasn't as heavy as before. On counting the money she found that there were only three thousand left!

"I'll give it back next week, I have to pay for the film," Ehsaan sahib smiled. The Begum understood that he had taken his commission.

"But ..."

"Why are you worrying so much?" he said, speaking like a husband. "The sari-wallah is coming in the evening."

"All you can talk about are saris when I have a thousand other expenses to think of."

"Just wait and see what happens. Allah is a great helper, everything will be taken care of. And I'll be making arrangements for the flat today. When will you be able to shift?"

"What do I have to take with me? I'll buy new furniture when I get there."

"Why buy new furniture? The furniture from my last palace set is sitting in the studio. It's ultra modern. I'll tell the seth, he'll have it delivered to the flat."

"But ...

"But what?"

"Masooma!"

"She's very young and doesn't know anything. You'll have to explain it to her firmly."

Explain? How could she explain? When the girl had reached puberty she had been too embarrassed to say anything to her. She had entrusted the task to Baqri bua. Her aunt was the one who had raised her, she was the one who had explained everything.

Baqri bua. What a stroke of good luck that she was no longer alive. She would always pester the girls:

"Oi girl, cover your head with the dupatta – do respectable daughters and daughters-in-law roam around with their heads uncovered?"

No girl ever dared to speak in a loud voice:

"Speak softly child; strange men can hear your voice!"

If she had been here ...! But there was no Baqri bua – no nawabi grandeur – there was nobody!

Masooma Bano was petulantly scratching off nail polish from the little finger of her left hand. Ahmad bhai had gone to Surat for a few days. By the time he returned the swelling on his eye had subsided and a scab had formed over the wound on his nose. And sitting next to her, he was making a list of items of furniture. He looked up at her and shamelessly bared his teeth in a smile. Irritated she stood up and walked out to the other room. When the truck arrived all the rubbish in the house was piled onto it. Everyone sat in Ahmad bhai's car. He tried to make Masooma sit next to him, but she bristled and moved away from the car. The Begum broke into a laugh, sent Saleem to sit in the front with Ahmad bhai, and brought her to sit with her in the back.

"What is this rude behaviour?" she said lovingly as she rearranged a lock of hair over Masooma's forehead.

Masooma impatiently pushed away her hand.

"By God, I'll give you such a slap your teeth will fall out. You're becoming more and more spoilt, you wretch."

While the truck was being unloaded at the flat, Masooma stood quietly in a corner, detached from everything and everyone.

"I made a mistake, baba, please, forgive me," Ahmad bhai said, coming up to her.

Masooma scrunched up her nose.

"If you want me to, I'll do push-ups, I'll hold my nose, I'll say salaam three times. I made a mistake. Here, look, I'm holding my ears." He grabbed his ears.

Masooma started laughing either at the sight of his silly face or at her own helplessness. The Begum tried to explain.

"Look how much he's doing for us. The rent alone for this place is two hundred and fifty rupees."

"So let's go back to the old house then – the rent there was only seventy rupees."

"And who will pay that seventy?" the mother asked, and then Masooma understood. Her anger vanished. The same old laughter and jokes began to resound once again. After all, who can resist the allure of beautiful clothes and jewellery? She held out with as much force as she was capable of and then gave in. After all she wasn't so naïve as to be unaware of the value of her existence.

Then one day Ahmad bhai finally received his payment. And Masooma Bano became Nilofar. The Begum's grand ways saw a return – the same abundance of food, the same line of servants. Saleem mian was immediately enrolled in the best school, and a chauffeur-driven car dropped him off and picked him up. The Begum now left her bed around eleven in the morning as she had done before. It was as if she had been having a bad dream and had woken up to find that nothing had changed. The only difference was that Nawab sahib was not there any more, but did Ehsaan sahib not make enough of a fuss over her? As someone had once said, he was now harvesting his field. The deep well he had been digging all these years had finally yielded the sweetest water for him to drink. There had been a time when the Begum would sometimes treat him badly, but now he was eating all his meals with her. His wife and daughter had also been drawn into the Begum's social circle. The two women were convinced that Ehsaan sahib's relationship with the Begum was no more than one that might exist between an unfortunate woman and her husband's acquaintance and friend. He was considerate of everyone's needs. The Begum began spending money open-handedly. She wouldn't think twice before buying Banarasi saris and gold jewellery as birthday gifts for just about anyone.

Anyway, now they were both at the age when they actually couldn't be anything more than a brother and sister to each other. The Begum was indebted to him. Who else did the poor woman have except him? Who else would have safely brought her boat ashore? If he asked her for something, she gave generously. But as for Ahmad bhai, he didn't seem too happy. Nilofar behaved like a spoilt sweetheart and made him dance to her tune. When he arrived, she started playing carom or cards with the kids. If he asked her to come to the bedroom, she made excuses. When the Begum did finally manage to send her in, she would start quarrelling with him, find reasons to argue, scratch like a cat and then run off to her mother. Ahmad bhai hovered, tried to appease her and gave her bribes but, unmoved, she still managed to dodge him. Ahmad bhai had never spent the night there. His father-in-law had given him strict orders: go where you want, but at night, sleep at home. So at twelve, like Cinderella, he had to run. If Nilofar was in a good mood she sat down and had a few drinks with him, uttered expletives, and then resorted to punching him. And then suddenly, as if possessed by a jinn, she would command him to bark like a dog. The poor fellow had no choice but to bark. Then she would clap gleefully, throw her shoe across the room and order him, "Crawl on all fours, bark and then pick up the shoe with your teeth and bring it to me, bark again and put the shoe on my foot." If he was in the right mood, Ahmad bhai would bark loudly, pick up the shoe with his teeth and bring it to her, and then she would throw it again. Sometimes, in front of everyone, she would order him to bray like a donkey.

"Not right now, later," he would say.

"No, do it now."

"I said not now, I'll do it later. Give me a little kiss first."

"No, bray like a donkey right now, this very minute."

"Are you out of your mind, you impertinent creature?" the Begum would scold her.

"Nobody interfere," Nilofar would snap stubbornly. "Amma, please keep quiet."

"It looks like you're going to get into trouble," the Begum would roar.

But Ahmad bhai would say, "It's a lover's game, why do you get in the way?" And then he would proceed to bray like a donkey. But by now Nilofar would be in a bad mood and would make him submit to the worst possible indignities. Sometimes Ahmad bhai complained to Ehsaan sahib. He was tired now. He was at an age when he should have been the beloved, his wife and children should have been waiting on him, giving him respect and obedience.

What a strange place this world is! One day when Ehsaan sahib returned after a week of outdoor shooting with Saman, he found his house empty. His wife had eloped with his very dependable private secretary, the man he had regarded as a brother. The neighbours had taken pity on his two girls and given them refuge. The younger boy she had left with her sister, Apa. She told her sister she was going to the cinema. How much was there in the house? Everything had fitted on a truck. When Apa returned with the boy after a stroll at the seaside, she saw the two girls sitting in front of the house, bawling. All that remained inside the house were a few damaged utensils and some worthless pieces of furniture. His wife had carried off Ehsaan sahib's clothes too as a precaution. His clothes couldn't fit Mazhar who was very large and heavily built, while he was short and slight, but she took everything just to cause her husband as much aggravation as she could. She didn't leave behind even a grain of wheat.

It was strange that a woman who was a simple housewife would give up everything to run off with a man much younger than herself. But actually, Mazhar was not as young as he seemed. One of the reasons for his success was that he was deferential to anyone he met, immediately addressing them as "Bhai sahib." He had run away from home at the age of sixteen. The son of a degenerate nawab, he was able to survive in Bombay with the help of jewellery stolen from his mother and sisters. If he hadn't become attached to the toadies around him, he may have been able to lead a life of luxury for a while longer. But his friends and flatterers took him for such a wild ride that he soon became bankrupt. For many years he was busy with romantic liaisons, and along the way he picked up many addictions and quit as many more. When he finally came to his senses he found himself indentured to the fancies of an ageing heroine.

And then Mazhar came to terms with life. When his

ageing decrepit heroine abandoned him in favour of a younger man, Mazhar was devastated. Finally he landed the position of a stylish producer's toady. When someone who has been the object of toadyism himself has to turn around and become a toady, then there's no more to be said. He was now well versed in the subtle craft of toadyism. He had worked on several productions and had insinuated himself into the life of the person he worked with. Gradually he would start sleeping at his employer's house because after arranging a few late night parties, he would be too tired to go anywhere else. There was nothing he couldn't do. If, out of the blue, the producer wanted bird's milk or oxen's eggs, he would take a taxi and roam all over Bombay and eventually return with something even more bizarre. Wherever he lived, he became a member of the household. He would immediately cast the wife as a mother, sister, or sister-in-law and treat the mother-in-law as if he too were her son-in-law. He would help the unmarried sisters drown their sorrows, comfort the children while their father was away at work and sympathise with the wife as she grieved over her husband's frequent absences, absorbing her tears in his shirt-front. On the one hand he supplied his master with mistresses, on the other he applied balm to the wife's wounds caused by the burning flame of jealousy at these liaisons. If he addressed the wife as Apa, he immediately called the mistress Bhabi. And so everyone was happy with him. No matter what anyone asked him to do, he did it, whether it was fetching kebabs from Haji's hotel, or whisky from the Navy store, finding a singer from Pavanpul or making arrangements for a hunting trip, procuring raw film or stock shots – Mazhar untiringly supplied them all.

Whichever producer he attached himself to he would regard as God. He would sing his praises everywhere. Thanks to him the producer received such exposure that not even a penny had to be spent on publicity. Wherever he went he narrated tales of his sahib's intelligence, skill and expertise:

"Well, I say, sahib has done an amazing job. The shot was so wonderful, the cameraman went through contortions while taking it. What a picture. I swear the police will do everything they can to ban it but they won't succeed. Shantaram and Mehboob are nobodies compared to him!"

He also boasted about his master's faults:

"You see, the set's been standing for a whole month. There's shooting only maybe once a day. Four thousand feet of film was wasted on one song. And sahib is trying to get real marble for just two shots – and the floor won't even be visible in these close shots! But our sahib is adamant about the marble, because, you see, what he wants he has to have, otherwise he doesn't get into the right mood."

This was the reason why when a producer became bankrupt he passed Mazhar on to another producer as a legacy.

Ehsaan sahib had trusted Mazhar more than he trusted himself. He couldn't understand how such a virtuous wife and such a loyal friend could betray him like this. He passed several days in stunned silence. When Saman observed his condition, she was consumed with jealousy and began sulking. She complained about the bills at the Ritz Hotel, called Ehsaan sahib names, and then moved into the flat owned by the cloth merchant Moolchand in Khar that had been vacant for two months. Moolchand had just made a great deal of money by constructing flats on ownership. He was crazy about film stars and in his view Saman was also a film star.

Soon after his wife left Ehsaan sahib came down with a severe case of paratyphoid. The film accounts continued to be handled in a muddled sort of way, but the smaller receipts for the black money accounts had not yet been completed. Lenders had begun to threaten him, so he went underground in Lakheempur where his first wife lived.

Oh yes, this is the film line. Here there is a first wife

before the first wife. That's how this business works. Here love, marriage and business are all mixed up in the murky mess that is this industry. Anyone in films has to marry several times. The first wedding is that arranged by the parents when a person is still at a very young age. When the wife and children become a permanent blight and make it nearly impossible for him to enter his own house, then the man runs away to join films. If he happens to be living with his in-laws, then they begin to punish him for each morsel he gets from them. When the age to get a decent job passes, acquaintances begin to regard him as a debt-related disease.

But he recalls those famous film miracles: Mehboob was an extra; today he rules the film industry. Shantaram danced on the stage, Ashok Kumar earned fifty rupees a month as an assistant. All the successful and famous people had become something from nothing. And so, taking his wife's remaining jewellery, borrowing some suits from friends, procuring a suitcase and a holdall on loan, he starts off for Bombay.

After his arrival he stays in a hotel for a few days. Then, when his condition deteriorates, he dumps his luggage at someone's house and joins the ranks of freeloaders. He uses someone else's account for laundering his clothes, eats breakfast at another's house, and as for sleeping, he shacks up wherever he happens to be during a late-night event. Early in the morning he wakes up and goes to some studio, and attaches himself to some heroine or hero. These people tolerate him as a way to escape from their continuous boredom. They don't belong to any club, nor have they a place for entertainment, and no time to spend pursuing interests. People like him, who know how to flatter, are good company and help actors pass the time. After shooting is over for the day, every hero surrounds himself with such pigeons with trimmed wings, and proceeds to disparage other actors. Alcohol is the order of the day. The hopeful also gets to wet his throat. And so he gradually becomes the actor's toady.

During this time he promises his wife he will return soon and manages to convince her to sell more jewellery and send him the cash. When his shoes are completely worn out and his clothes are tattered, he does go back for a few days. But by then he has become used to life in Bombay and is addicted to the film world. He makes every effort to impress his family members with stories about his friendships. He talks in the hundreds and thousands, manages to wheedle money from here and there, and finally returns to Bombay.

If he is an effective flatterer, then, with the cooperation of a hero or heroine, he quickly assumes the role of a producer or a director. Acquiring a high-interest loan, he arranges a studio and raw film and then begs the hero or heroine to work for free for ten days. Either he himself becomes the director and producer, or he finds a penniless friend to get the film started. It would appear that he and the director don't make any profit, but if the film is a success, he thrives and lives comfortably until the funds from the film are depleted. But during this time he immediately has some new trousers and polyester shirts tailored, rents a flat and opens an office, bribes journalists and gains a great deal of publicity. Suddenly his status is elevated. Young men desirous of becoming heroes and young women accompanied by their mothers or grandmothers crowd around him. All day long he is thronged by people willing to work at no cost. Someone offers a free story, another insists on composing music without charging a penny. "You're giving that poet a thousand rupees for a song. I'm willing to write it for free. You can pay me when the song becomes a hit."

"Well, all I want is to see my name on the screen. Here's the story. You don't have to pay me anything."

Here one has to sell one's name to find work. So the clever producer sells the name of someone well known and has someone else do the actual work for a pittance. Now who has the guts to deal with the likes of him?

He also falls in love with an extra or an unsuccessful, aspiring heroine. Promising her work as a heroine in his next film, he gets the job done. If she is a patient, simple woman, he tolerates her for a while longer and then starts grooming another girl to become a heroine. Naturally, the girl he has accidentally turned into a heroine now immediately becomes virtuous and upright and begins making lakhs of rupees under the protection of her parents. If her film is a hit she breaks off relations with him.

That is why the moment a producer sees a vivacious young woman and likes her, he immediately corrals her and marries her. The young woman feels great pride in becoming a producer's wife. Until the day before she was being treated shabbily on the set, and today she is addressed as Begum sahib, and is ordering everyone around. Behind her back people speak of her in derogatory terms, but offer polite greetings to her face.

At one time Ehsaan sahib's wife had also been a permanent secondary heroine at Ranjeet. Usually she would be paired with the comedian in the comedy scenes. But people had long forgotten her. And she too, surrounded by children and housework, had turned into a dishevelled, ragged housewife. But, tired of Ehsaan sahib's continuous dalliances, she would also occasionally show an interest in someone else. Her relationship with Mazhar progressed over a long period of time. She knew Ehsaan sahib trusted her implicitly; she handled all the accounts. But she had been particularly irked by his romance with Saman, and so took the first chance she got to dump all the garbage on Ehsaan sahib's head, sweep the house clean of valuables, and elope with Mazhar.

And Ehsaan sahib couldn't do anything, because all the money had been generated by scams, and she was only his film wife. He had not felt the need to have a nikah. Who thought this ill-fated day would ever come?

The Begum was delighted at the news of the wife's departure. Good riddance. She had thought that Nilofar was a whore while she was a rich, good wife. How contemptuously she had spoken to her. There was something else. Ehsaan sahib was still receiving his commission and because the Begum no longer needed him, he was now a thorn in her side. She wanted to make a deal quietly and directly with Ahmad bhai. She had given Ehsaan sahib the cold shoulder many times, but he was as stubborn as a mule. He continued to laugh shamefacedly and didn't desist from taking the money. Such was his greed. His oven constantly demanded more and more fuel. He also wheedled money from other sources. Taking advantage of his absences, the Begum started talking about him behind his back. She constantly complained about him, demanded an account of every penny, and began exposing all his shady dealings.

How she had changed in these last few years. Her language had become coarse. If another woman even so much as looked at Ahmad bhai, she would react like a rival and burn with jealousy, uttering obscene curses. As for Nilofar, she already had nothing but contempt for Ahmad bhai, and now began to come down really hard on the man. Every sentence she spoke to him was accompanied by words like 'donkey,' or 'bastard cur' and so on. Now she didn't even flinch from picking up a shoe to smack him.

"You fool, why do you beat your livelihood with a shoe?" the Begum would ask fearfully. In her view Ahmad bhai was like a sack of flour with a perpetually open mouth that could always be dipped into. In addition to the monthly wages, he brought something or other every day. But Nilofar didn't pay any attention to his gifts.

"Is Baby never happy?" he would ask sorrowfully. He

called her Baby, the name reserved for film wives that seemed to boost their value.

"She's just pretending, Ahmad bhai. She doesn't want you to know, but she actually enjoys these games." The Begum spoke like a seasoned madam. Nature had taught her tricks necessary for her trade. She had put on a lot of weight. Her complexion had blossomed and resembled the colour of rose petals. She had also taken to using a great deal of make-up. In the past she had sometimes applied henna to her hair, but after she took Nilofar to the hairdresser and was told that she should dye her own hair, she began to use colour regularly. Her hair was thinning, but she looked much younger than her age. She felt no shame in having tight blouses stitched for herself, cut in a choli style with a tapering front that barely contained the big globs of flesh on her body. Her swollen, rounded fingers remained encased in rings and bands. When she sat down with a silver paan-daan in front of her and began making paans, all that was needed to complete the picture would be the humming of a sarangi and the beat of a tabla.

She had enrolled Saleem in St Peter's at Panchgani in the hills and she sent the girls there as well. The atmosphere in the house wasn't suitable for young children. Ahmad bhai and Nilofar's romance was like the squealing and roaring of cats and the children were beginning to sense what was happening. Nilofar used to break down doors. Then, drunk one day, Ahmad bhai committed an act that made Haleema hysterical. Crying, she ran and clutched her mother. Wearing just a flimsy towel around his waist, Ahmad bhai showed up to offer an explanation.

Waving his hands frantically, he said, "Such a bad girl, she is. Why peep into a private room? I didn't do anything. I just said, 'I'm doing something here, go and play in the veranda.' And then she says I grabbed her breast. Why would I grab her breast? Am I such a shameless man?"

He was appeased with much difficulty. And look at Nilofar! All she could do, the brazen girl, was break into giggles. The younger sister wasn't so young any more and understood a great deal. She knew very well what Ahmad bhai's relationship with Nilofar was. Ehsaan sahib also seemed to be overly nice to her and would drag her onto his lap every chance he had.

"Why waste time in school? Let her get dance lessons. I have very good connections with Nathu Maharaj," he would say and the Begum's blood would boil. She had already offered a sacrifice, but allowing the whole family to be involved was something she found abhorrent.

Nilofar was generally very careless, but when her sister and brother fell back in their studies she yelled at them. Sometimes, when she was holding their books in her hands, she would lovingly rifle through the pages as if searching in them for that lost time when she also attended school. How much fun they had in those days! How she would huddle with her friends and talk about life, love and romance and giggle about their throbbing virginal dreams that were filled with the aroma of ubtan, rich with the colour of henna and the fragrance of the bridal package. She would get lost in the silent melody of the wedding flutes that would never play. And then she would be startled – Ahmad bhai's slobbering lips were crushing her virginal being and she would grab whatever was closest and throw it at him. She had become very reckless. One day, in the midst of a bout of teasing, she kicked Ahmad bhai where she shouldn't have and he yelped like a slaughtered goat. He walked down the stairs with great difficulty. The next day he doubled up in pain and collapsed. He was immediately taken to the hospital and was discovered to have suffered a strangulation of the hernia. The slightest carelessness could have ended his life.

He stayed at the Waccha Nursing Home for two weeks. Every day he clamoured to see Nilofar. She would come after a great deal of fuss and start quarrelling with him. During his recovery his father-in-law began to tighten his purse strings. The money he had invested in films was lost. It became difficult to pay the hospital bill. The Begum sat coiled around what she had like a snake. What did she really have? There were too many expenses. Five hundred was just the fees for the children's schools. And every other day she also sent them parcels. And there were the ongoing feasts at the house as well.

Ehsaan sahib had returned from the house of his in-laws. He had broken up with Ahmad bhai and he too had no money now. The person who owned the world rights for the half-finished film had taken possession of the office. Ahmad bhai had been issuing IOUs everywhere. The distributors were demanding delivery of the film. Maganlal dress-wallah had sued as well. Ehsaan sahib had made three flops one after another and was now all tied up in debt.

How the Begum had warned that idiotic girl Nilofar to buy jewellery and not waste money on rubbish. But she had been so stubborn and showed no interest in anything except those black and yellow saris. And when did she ever wear those saris? She would roam around in the house dressed in a shabby housecoat all day. The Begum had tried to tell her many times to dress well and look attractive but she didn't heed her.

And who came to her aid at this difficult time? Ehsaan sahib! He brought Surajmal over to visit them.

When Ahmad bhai heard about it, he threw a fit. He became hysterical and threatened to shoot Surajmal.

"Are you out of your mind?" the Begum said. "He was here for only a few minutes and then he left. I swear by God, he's such a respectable man. He didn't even look at Baby in a bad way, let alone hold her hand."

"You rogues, so dishonest you are. I'm sick for a few days

and you get another seth working for you. All of you are thieves."

"You are not being reasonable. The poor man visited us at a difficult time while you were hiding inside your wife's bosom. You wouldn't have cared if we had been ruined."

"What is this nonsense? When did I hide inside my wife's bosom? I only went back to get my stuff. I'll give her a divorce if you want. We'll have a nikah, right away, so we can stop all this babble."

"Nikah?" The Begum broke into a loud laugh. "Seth, when it was time to have the nikah and we grovelled at your feet for it, what kind of a dismissive reply did you give? 'I don't want to get involved in this hassle.' Well, God saved my daughter, because I, stupid fool, was ready to dump her into the fire myself."

"But I'm saying that I'll have the nikah, and whatever else you want."

"So ask Nilofar. If she's ready I don't care." The Begum knew what Nilofar would say, but she wanted to fan the flames.

"No, no. She's so moody. That's why I'm asking you."

"Why you asking me?" she said, screwing up her face, mocking his lingo.

"You're her *guarjian*," he said.

"Oh my, why should I be her *guarjian*?" she mimicked his accent. "God bless her, she's not a little girl any more. She makes her own decisions. She'll do what she wants. She can have ten nikahs if she wants – I don't care."

"That girl, she's like a hurricane."

"I'm not getting involved. She's in her room, you can go and talk to her yourself."

Ahmad bhai crept nervously up to Nilofar's room. Dressed in a magenta-coloured brocade housecoat, she was sprawled on the floor, one thigh exposed. Today Ahmad bhai shut the door.

"Baby," he said fearfully. Golden hairs shone on her ivory-coloured calf, resembling a white kundan designed by an expert craftsman.

"Baby darling," he muttered pleadingly.

"What is it?" she asked from behind a magazine.

"How are you?"

"I'm fine. Why?" After living in his company for so long she had got into the habit of speaking like him.

"Are you angry with me?"

"Why?" She again imitated his speech.

"Then why you don't give me a kiss?"

"You want a kiss? Here, take a kiss." She pursed her lips and thrust her chin at him. But when Ahmad bhai leaned forward she quickly rolled away from him and with a jolt the poor fellow landed flat on his face. The doctor had asked him to be careful.

Exhausted, sweating profusely, Ahmed bhai retreated down the stairs with trembling legs and lowered head. Nilofar's laughter pursued him with a clapping sound.

"Why did he leave so soon?" the Begum asked.

"He blew a fuse." Nilofar cackled loudly, like someone driven insane. She laughed so much that her eyes began to water.

"Are you mad?" The Begum pushed the children out of the room and covered Nilofar's body with a blanket. But when Nilofar told her the story between attacks of laughter, the Begum couldn't resist a smile.

"Oh my, you're very cruel," she said.

"Why? What was I supposed to do?" Nilofar threw off the blanket, "It's so hot."

The Begum had given birth to Nilofar. Until only a few years ago she would occasionally give her a bath herself. But now, seeing her naked youthful body sprawled on the wrinkled bedspread, she shuddered. It was as if someone had taken her and forced her to stand naked on a street corner. Fate had battered and pounded the Begum, but she still had some shame left. Ehsaan sahib was not related to her, but in the days when she was young she hadn't even allowed her husband to keep the light on. And Nilofar's profession entailed darkness. The sight of her burnished body under the light of a hundred kilowatt bulb was making the Begum flush with shame.

"Get up, you shameless wretch! Stop lolling about like a wild bull."

"But I'm so hot." She stretched again.

The Begum came out and shut the door behind her. She caught Saleem trying to peep through the window and walloped him. He was home for a fifteen-day break and was miserable at the thought of having to return to school.

THREE

WHEN EHSAAN SAHIB HAD RETURNED it seemed as if he had been sick for a long time. He was extremely frail; his hair was dry and drab since he had stopped colouring it; his complexion had taken on a muddy, lifeless look; his clothes were shabby. His woman and his secretary had left him with nothing. If his real wife had some money, she wasn't willing to spend it on him. He returned from there empty-handed and empty-hearted. He could depend on the Begum for meals, but she too had taken to reminding him again and again that he had already received his commission. As for Ahmad bhai, ever since his return from the hospital after being kicked by Nilofar and his last unfortunate encounter with her, he had become somewhat stingy. Nilofar showed little interest except in making fun of everything. The rent was accumulating, as were Saleem's expenses and their lives would be made intolerable if the girls' fees were not paid by the tenth. So many expenses and all she had was an income of only fifteen hundred to two thousand rupees.

Ehsaan sahib had no alternative but to head out to some studio or the other every morning. There he would settle down in the make-up room of an artist he knew well and proceed to dig the grave of some unfortunate producer. After breakfast he would follow the same artist to the set. Many people still had no idea about his actual condition. At one time he had been a producer and so he would still be surrounded by small time extras:

"Well Ehsaan sahib, when are you starting the picture?"

"I'm just about to have an opening ceremony. Yesterday I made a deal with Dev Anand, and Sunil Dutt likes the role as well. It's a double role. A rich boy and a poor boy, both look-alikes. I say, it's a great story. Rajinder Singh Bedi has agreed to write the dialogues. Don't tell anyone, the story is actually by Mukhram Sharma, but for some reason he wants to keep his name out."

Those who knew him guessed immediately that it was all a fabrication, but those who didn't would start making a fuss over him, especially when he announced:

"I want a new girl to be the heroine."

All the relatives of the new girls immediately surrounded him as if he were Raja Indar.

"Bring tea for Ehsaan sahib. Here, have a cigarette. There's a girl, would you like to see her? Forget Vyjantimala and Meena Kumari. Lachoo Maharaj has trained her himself. Actually, no one can equal him in Kathak in all of Hindustan. I say, Ehsaan sahib, what a girl she is!"

"Who is she?"

"You'll see her. Arrange for a test."

"Are you talking about Sarita?"

"No, no, what are you talking about? Her father is a troublemaker. The other day he showed up drunk at Narayan sahib's set and began cursing, accusing the director of asking her to come for rehearsals just to aggravate him. She was not called for the actual shooting, he said, the director was using rehearsals just as an excuse to get close to her."

"Don't you know, he's not her father?"

"But we had heard he is married to her mother."

"Married? So what? Yes, he is married to her mother, but she's inconsequential. The woman used to play the heroine opposite Master Wathal in silent films. At first he used to follow Sarita around. She got him work several times, but he has always been a troublemaker. He would ruin relationships wherever he went. And on the day of the shooting he would start making a fuss. He was thrown out from every place he went to."

Suddenly, Ehsaan sahib turned around. "Oh, welcome, welcome, Madam. We never see you any more."

Dressed as a Balochi damsel, five feet two inches tall with the aid of high heels, Sarita was approaching them. The moment they saw her, all those who had been disparaging her immediately changed their tune and began heaving the lovelorn sighs of loyal devotees. This is the film world. Everything here is artificial. There are special plasters available to turn white to black and black to white, there are wigs for bald heads, and rubber caps for heads with hair to give them the bald look. Apply make-up along flat, broad noses to turn them into thin, fine noses, and tinsel and sparkles to small, dark eyes to make them come alive. If the hair is dull and drab, use Ganga One for a long braid twirling down the back in no time, and long hair can be rolled up to look bobbed. If the mouth is small, apply lipstick generously and make the lips fuller, if it is too big, narrow the line of lipstick. If the heroine is thin and scrawny get her rubber hips and a bust from a high-class chemist's shop, if she's fat – which most successful heroines are after a few films – then dress her in tight clothes, wrap her in elastic belts and take camera shots to make her appear thin as a stick. If she's short make her stand on a six-inch high stool, if she's too tall then have special elevated shoes made for the hero. Avoid having the tall heroine stand alongside the hero, keeping her at his feet most of the time so that the hero appears gigantic – like our dear Raj Kapoor does with Nutan.

Talk slipped away from Sarita and turned to the make-up box. The same people who had been calling her names changed their colours like a chameleon. That's the safest course of action. The person who functions as your doorman today could suddenly be your producer tomorrow and become your caretaker. Not the big-time producers of course, but those minor producers who depend on some influential personage for their status; crows who hover around some famous star and are converted to producers so that the star can turn black money into white. Actually, films are made in their name so that that the stars can avoid paying income tax. Everyone in the film industry knows this. Even the distributor knows who the real owner of the film is and who is just the cover.

On the surface it would appear that these cover-producers don't get wages for their services. Whatever they can manage to swindle is their payment. This cover-producer is a very useful person. In name he is a producer and owns everything, but like the King of England he has all the rights and still has nothing, and this producer is made to sign away everything he has as collateral. Unfortunately he cannot commit the tiniest bit of fraud. If the film is a hit the real owner takes everything, and if it's a flop, the cover is rendered ineffective for the rest of his life.

This cover-producer is usually of great use, although he's generally penniless. Using his influence, begging and pleading with artists, he's able to make them reduce their fees. The real producer, who holds a special position, can't do the begging and keeps his head high while the cover gets all the work done.

Once again the conversation turned to Sarita. But why

talk about her? Let's forget Sarita. She's changed her name many times, but there's nothing these names can do if she doesn't have it in her to be successful. She was short, with skin like a mottled chicken, and if she hadn't been in films she could have been washing dishes somewhere and no one would be clamouring for her autograph. Seeing her in the film world makes one believe in God's plan. If she were not acting in films, she would have by now delivered many daughters who would have looked just like her and done nothing to elevate the nation's standards of beauty. By remaining unmarried she is doing our race a big favour. But she's already married! Now it seems to the man who was once her mother's lover!

Just then Ahmed bhai arrived on the scene. For some time now his relationship with Ehsaan sahib had been one of fire and water. The presence of one didn't leave space for the other. Ehsaan sahib was about to slip away quietly when Ahmad bhai snagged him and dragged him behind the sets.

"I already told you Ahmed bhai, you can't manage this girl."

"The girl is no good, what can I do?"

"Seth, it isn't the girl who is no good. Perhaps you're the one who is no good?" Ehsaan sahib became angry.

"What do you mean? Bombay's best girls are available to me."

"They must be the prostitutes who ply their trade on Pavanpul. Seth, this one is from a good family. It was my mistake. One should check the customer before dispensing the goods. And you gave our friendship –"

"Why do you lose your cool?"

"Because you say such ludicrous things. What is this? The girl kicks you and you land in the hospital for two weeks?"

"Then what shall I do? Tell me. Her mother trusts you and listens to you."

"My goodness, you've actually lost your sanity. What will her mother do? Of course if you want the mother ..."

"What nonsense is this? I don't like this kind of a joke."

"So what can I do? I'm quite worried myself. These women ..." Ehsaan sahib heaved a long sigh. "All right seth, I have to go, I have some things to take care of."

"Listen to me. What kind of a man are you?"

"Look seth, I have an appointment. I have to read a story to Dev. The signing money is ready, shooting starts next month."

"Are you trying to fool me?"

"I don't have to, I'm observing God's handiwork. He has made this one with His own hands."

"What?"

"Let it be, you won't understand."

"Have you made any arrangement about my money?"

"I will, it will happen. I have to be going now. If you know of a second-hand car then ..." Ehsaan sahib tried to evade the issue.

"You want a car?"

"It's tough without a car."

"If you have money for a bloody car, how come you don't have anything to pay me?" Ahmed bhai thundered.

"Oh, I'm not getting a car for myself. You know Deepchand, don't you, Surajmal's brother-in-law, he's the one who needs a car." Ehsaan sahib quickly turned his story around.

"I know what you're up to. You're trying to get a car in his name, but it's really for yourself. Under whose name are you starting the company?"

"I have a nephew, he ..."

"What's this fraud? One company collapses, and in no time another company starts. All right, don't worry, I'll get even with you soon. I won't rest until you're insolvent."

"You know, seth, I've been insolvent for four years. You gave the money to Ghulam Rasul, and now you're asking me for it."

"You gave me Ghulam Rasul's name, you said you would return the money."

"You're venting your anger at the girl on me. If you ask me, seth, you should grind almonds and eat them. God willing ..."

"What almonds? Oh, those things give me diarrhoea." Ahmad bhai spoke so wistfully that Ehsaan sahib couldn't help breaking into a laugh.

"I said silence! Who is this rascal talking behind the sets? Kick him out. How long it has taken for this shot and now it's ruined. Oh! Ehsaan sahib, it's you. I'm sorry."

But after Ehsaan sahib said, "It's all right" and left, the director proceeded to curse him heavily. "What a scoundrel! He promised to take me as director and made me run after him for a whole year, and then I find he's penniless."

Moments earlier he had been cursing the entire industry in Ehsaan sahib's company.

"No, sahib, this film line is not for the respectable. Only prostitutes and reprobates can get ahead here."

It would seem that Ehsaan sahib himself was an angel. Actually he had been going around saying that this very director had gained prominence with the help of his wife's commendations, and if he didn't get what he wanted he would insist on forcing his conjugal rights on his wife.

This director also had a very interesting background. Both he and his wife belonged to a class of well-educated people and had been working in amateur theatre just as a hobby. No one knows who advised them to go into films: "The Ganga is flowing, you take a dip into it as well." And they came. They stayed with various friends for a while, met with groups interested in art, people who could help them with work but not with making money. How long can hospitality last in Bombay? So they started to look for real work. The wife would go to a producer, recount her tale of woe and cry on his shoulder and obtain a little work for her husband. Often with some effort, she was able to have this extended. Some people claimed she developed spiritual friendships, but who in the film industry believes in jinns and witches? The husband develops an inferiority complex and begins to feel that he is only known because of his wife. So he starts quarrelling with her and makes life hell for her. He meddles in whatever film she's working on, accuses her of carrying on with the entire staff, and declares that he is going to give everyone a beating. Once again the wife, after a psychological analysis of her husband, rests her head on the chests of her platonic sympathisers and weeps. In the meantime, the husband maintains his threatening stance, but the moment he gets work, he embarks on a love affair with the heroine or the supporting heroine. If the cast is A-rated, then he is satisfied with the dancer or the back-up dancer. His wife becomes jealous and again goes to her romantic friends in tears. Allah has buried springs of never-drying tears in her eyes.

These days the director's romance with Sarita is at its height. His Begum sahiba is currently drowning in misery. If this had been a high-class heroine instead of Sarita, she wouldn't feel such shame but falling for a low-rated actress spells nothing but disaster. If a director is romantically involved with a first-class heroine then he can be sure he has acquired the keys to the bank reserves. The heroine cannot be invited to the most important soirees until he receives an invitation first. He can start ten companies and become the grandest of producers. All the money earned in black is his anyway, but he can also devour every penny of the white. Whatever she earns he can spend freely or save in his name. When she grows old, he can ensnare a new bird. These first-rate heroines who heave long hot sighs in the romantic film scenes are prone to dive into dry sand. The world leers at them lustfully, but no one will love them. Once they get married, they cannot escape from the husband's clutches. And if they do escape, they flee from the frying pan only to fall into the fire. If it's a low-class girl, the financier won't even let her touch him. And Sarita, although in real life might be a flame, a spark, looked like a bombal fish onscreen. But any third-rate producer she supported did manage to get some financing from somewhere.

At this moment a dance of hers was being filmed. In order to lure the hero toward a path of wrongdoing she was using every trick at her command. There was gambling in progress at the café and, arching her body, she was going up to everyone, biting her lips and jiggling her breasts. But, for the extras on the set, her actions were like the "*khat, khat*" of a machine. No one was aroused by her performance. After working with a machine for a long period of time, a person also turns into a machine. Extreme heat, dust, melting make-up and working without pay – the artists in this film had been hired on the condition that they would receive payment only when the film made money – all of this had deadened their hearts and dulled their emotions.

But people were making obscene comments. Sarita's skirt was very full and when she spun like a top, her dark pink panties shimmered like a red flag. The assistant was sitting below the camera putting the shot number and date on the clapper. The hairdresser, after a glass of lassi, was now chewing paan and was on hand to remove the pins and curlers and set the hair properly before the final rehearsal. The producer owes everyone. Regardless of whether the scene calls for loose hair, the hairdresser is required to be present, and because she is also Nargis and Madhubala's hairdresser, she is brought in by every two-bit actress. She spends less time doing hair and more performing the role of an ayah and is privy to all the gossip about everyone in the industry. The more difficult a heroine is, the more bad-tempered her hairdresser, especially since she also acts as her messenger and her confidante. She helps her conduct romantic liaisons, delivers her missives, listens to the sad stories of relatives – mothers, grandmothers and husbands – who regard the heroine as a money-making machine, and even accompanies the heroine to the bathroom.

When the producer noticed the assistants sitting on their haunches, deeply engrossed in the view, he also bent down and catching a glimpse of the shimmer and sparkle of the panties, became furious.

"There will be no such obscenity on my set," he roared. "All of you are sitting here, watching like asses. The censors will knock off this shot. Go and get some proper underwear for her."

Sarita was dismayed when she heard this.

The assistants came up with words of support. In such and such film the panties were even skimpier and also skin-coloured so that the girl looked naked. The director became annoyed. He knew why the film featuring the naked-looking girl had escaped the censor's scissors. That producer was always able to save the most objectionable things in his films. Anyone who has friends in high places can save anything and the censor's scissors sneak past the scenes not cutting a single frame. It's the small-time producers who get into trouble and dread the censor's scissors, just as a calf dreads the butcher's knife. And what a knife – like a blind bull's horns that come at you randomly.

What a horrible scene it is. The censor trial is in progress inside and outside the producer is tormented with diarrhoea. For a whole month he has been running himself ragged trying to finalise the editing. When will the film be completed? No one has been paid in full. Begging, using his wife and children as bait, somehow he manages to finish the film. Except for the editor, the director and the two assistants, no one has any more work to do. Everyone's interest has waned except the distributor who is threatening to crucify him. At last the editing is done, he has managed to get hold of some background music from here and there and puts it in, and finally the corpse is adorned and placed before the censors. It is like making your daughter sit in the marriage bower. The exhibitor is threatening to spend the advance if the picture isn't handed over right away and the producer is pulling the noose tighter by saying the payments will have to be returned if the film is not delivered on time. A criminal case will be brought against him. Meanwhile the lenders from the previous film are bullying him so that the moment a single droplet trickles down they can seize it. And as for the censors, poised with scalpels in hand, they are bent over the corpse.

The film's fate is decided. Only three thousand feet of film have to be cut. Two songs are dispatched to heaven. Two songs are wounded so badly that plastic surgery may leave them moaning for life. Dialogue and words are randomly selected for deletion from here and there.

There, the film is finally censored. A big fight only results in a deal similar to one made between two roadside vendors: it's neither mine nor yours, we each get half. Only one thousand, five hundred feet of film has been cut, and now there's preparation underway for another attack. Another committee is shown the film and it comes out unharmed, with only three or four hundred feet of bad stuff taken out, and finally passes. But if a very influential personage is present on the revising committee, then the film might be banned altogether. No one can trust the censors. Everything is in the hands of blind fate. If an arrow does not hit its mark, at least it's a near miss. One will hear that a certain film has been banned and then suddenly the news will arrive that the film almost received the President's award and it's now being given prizes at various film festivals.

"I'm hot." Sarita Devi was not ready to relinquish the panties. She could see the illuminating shine on the faces of the people on the set. If these people are suddenly breathless, how will the public react? Won't they just die? These directors were the actresses' enemies – they deliberately wasted their sex appeal. The truth of the matter was that Sarita Devi was being cut so mercilessly by the censors that the directors had begun to view her as a threat to the film. And as for the viewers, if they happened to see even one shot of her shaking her hips, wiggling her shoulders, or shuddering as she chewed her lips, they would become hysterical – that film was generally a hit. People showered her with thousands of rupees just to see the jiggling of her breasts.

"Okay, so let's take a close shot today." The director decided to overlook the situation.

When the camera came down a little more for the close shot, she lowered her body and then thrust her chest forward so suggestively that the cameraman became flustered.

"It won't work."

"What won't work, you fool?" The director asked, irritated.

"Why don't you take a look first – and then say what you want. I don't care. But think about it."

"OK, move over," the director said, looking into the camera. "A little to the left – there, that's it – a little to the right – stop, stop – what?" The director looked into the camera, then up at the assistant, then at Sarita Devi, and then he started scratching his head.

"Lights off." The lights were shut down. The make-up man was summoned.

"Sahib, I don't know anything, ask the dress-wallah," he said.

"What do you mean?"

"Sahib, I tried to talk her out of it, but she wouldn't listen."

"What do you mean?"

"You know Qamar – well, she took them."

"So what? Don't we have any more panties among our costumes?"

"Yes we do sahib, but not in size one. Those are the only size we have. The *Stroll in Fairyland* guys had taken what we had. When they were returned they were not the same, they were size two. I went there after the shoot yesterday. They said, 'They're in the property somewhere, come some other time and exchange them.'"

"But we can't use these size two ones." The director wouldn't budge.

"All right then, take a back shot," said the producer trying to appease him.

"Call for make-up."

Sarita Devi began preparations for a back shot.

Nilofar was dreaming of the girl who was once Masooma, who had played with dolls and been afraid of the dark, who would put up a swing on the neem tree during the rainy season and climb up high on it, who had memorised innumerable verses and whose group always won the poetry recitation competitions, and who had played the role of Ophelia in the school play, making the audience weep uncontrollably.

She had adored Shelley and loved Keats with a passion. Her heart would beat violently at the very mention of Byron's name. Whatever she had read and understood was enough to make her surrender her heart to them. Her father would say "We'll send Chooma to England." If only she had completed her Senior Cambridge! But these were just dreams. Very lively dreams, which Masooma Bano was still suspended in.

But Nilofar had slipped out of this net. She chewed on chocolates and toffees. She played screaming, howling rumba-samba records and slept on Dunlop pillows. She was surrounded by *True Story*, *True Romance* and confections designed for different kinds of women. Her body was rapidly filling out.

"What is this?" the Begum said, slapping her on her naked rump.

"Oh ... I'm so hot." She pulled up a corner of the sheet and pretended to cover herself and began chewing a large piece of chocolate. Children from the neighbourhood were peeping through the front window. The Begum had shooed them off a while ago.

"So what are your plans now?" the Begum asked, picking up clothes from the chair and throwing them on the bed to make room for herself. She plonked herself on the chair. She too had put on more weight in the last few months.

"The last notice has just arrived from Panchgani," she continued.

"You didn't send the money yet?"

"Where was I going to get the money? This is the third month a payment has been missed."

"Payment for what?" Nilofar asked dreamily. She was at a very interesting point in her story. The man who had raped the heroine and made her pregnant was about to envelop her in his strong arms and propose marriage.

"I say, may these books burn," the Begum said, trying to snatch the book from her hands. Nilofar quickly hid it under the sheet and started laughing.

"You shameless girl. Always reading filthy books. They've turned you into a good-for-nothing. I swear one day I'll put them all together and burn them."

"Oh ... why?"

"You stupid girl! Have you ever thought of what will happen if Ahmad bhai slips through our fingers?"

Nilofar laughed foolishly. She had stopped thinking a long time ago.

"So what can I do?"

"Who did you go with to Varsoda the other day?"

"No one."

"And to make matters worse, now you're lying." The Begum grabbed her hair and pulled her face toward her. Nilofar yanked herself free. Her constant wrestling with Ahmad bhai had taught her these moves.

"Well, I went with Manohar. Who else would I go with?" She lifted her hand to push back her hair and the sheet fell down. Her shamelessness angered the Begum. Afraid of her mother's wrath, Nilofar quickly covered herself with her dressing gown.

"Have you no shame? You go off like a whore with anyone who comes along."

The Begum had come to tell Nilofar to take pity on Ahmad bhai, and traipsing around with Manohar was proof of her wantonness! Manohar, the son of schoolmaster living next door was in his second year at college, and used to wave to Nilofar from his window.

How sad all this was for Nilofar! Manohar was a few years younger than her. A thin, lean, wiry boy. While playing cricket in the maidan he would notice Nilofar at the window and start showing off his manliness.

His window was adjacent to Nilofar's. She often pushed her curtain aside. He generally sat with a book in hand and pretended to read while Nilofar roamed freely about in her room. Manohar would gape at her. The book would fall from his hands but even then he would not come out of his trance.

One day Nilofar purposely threw down her hairbrush

with the silver handle and then bent down to see where it had fallen. Manohar darted down the stairs like an arrow. When he arrived in Nilofar's room with the brush, the Begum was out visiting someone in the neighbourhood. She was the one who had left the door ajar.

When she returned and saw the open door and the two of them sharing a plate of roasted peas, she took the same brush and smacked Manohar so hard on his butt that he ran out. Nilofar laughed until she was out of breath. The scene was so funny that she couldn't stop herself. The Begum's eyes bulged with wrath. With the same brush in hand, she went toward Nilofar who jumped away and leapt onto the window. The Begum knew that if she moved any closer, Nilofar would jump down onto the neighbour's roof in her unseemly garb. People had already begun to complain about their unsavoury behaviour. This was an area inhabited for the most part by people from the film world and every other day there was some commotion. Feeling helpless, she fell into a chair and began to cry.

The Begum found herself worrying that Nilofar was not dressing properly, that her weight was increasing, and that if she continued in this way her youthfulness would wane in a few years. She was becoming experienced so rapidly – how quickly and how easily evil becomes part of a person's being. So many avatars and prophets struggled, lost, and relinquished their lives while trying to teach lessons of goodness; evil is interesting and exciting while goodness is like chewing tough metallic marbles.

But this was not the fault of evil or goodness. The fault lay with the artificial society in which she had been raised. There was fasting, namaz, Haj and zakat – but there was also whoring and vice carried out in secrecy. The transgressions one commits may be hidden from society, but they can't be hidden from one's offspring. The Hazoor-e-Aala had many wives, slaves, mistresses. Was it possible for him, a nawab, to keep all of them happy? But all were alive and in human shape. The daughters did not get married. Were they all virgins? As for the many children born in one year in his old age, did anyone else except their mothers know who their fathers were?

Perhaps it was Aala Hazrat's good sense that made him do it, or perhaps he was naturally stingy, but he had recently announced in the estate gazette that he was extremely old and any children now born in the palace should not be considered his.

All the vices characteristic of the feudal system had been lying dormant, but because of the starvation and poverty experienced by the Begum, these vices had been revived. If the Begum had been shackled by the weaknesses of a middle-class mentality, she would have survived by stitching clothes instead of selling her daughter. The girl would have been able to obtain a minor teaching position in some school. If they had managed to be frugal even the jewellery would have gone a long way. But they were not used to a hard life and had not seen anyone lead a hard life either. True, girls had been traded for generations. Their young aunt had been married off to that doddering old Nawab Qamaruddin for his money. Everyone knew she had had a relationship with the Civil Surgeon sahib. The nawab's older daughter's husband had married a white woman. She in turn had sought solace in the arms of a poet. Honour and respectability were weighed on the scales of money and status.

And what great sin had she committed anyway that she should feel remorseful? And who in Bombay asks who you are or how you make a living. Is there anyone there who can look at himself and say he is a unique individual who has never pimped for anything?

The Begum knew that Nilofar saw Manohar behind her

back, took him everywhere with her, and spent money on him. If she had developed this obsession late in life, it would be different, but the Begum had never seen anyone play with kids like this while still in the fullness of youth.

When, tying her waistband, Nilofar came out of the bathroom, the Begum began scolding her again.

"I'll marry Manohar," Nilofar responded.

The Begum recoiled as though bitten by a snake.

"You'll marry him? And what will you eat? His father will feed you? Are you crazy?"

Their squabbling continued for hours. The Begum wept, then Nilofar wept, and finally the Begum's tears triumphed and Nilofar promised that she would not see Manohar again. The Begum had a sneaking suspicion this wasn't going to be easy. She ran into Manohar's father at the dentist's clinic and hinted: "Your son isn't paying attention to his studies, and he also wastes my daughter's time. Please do something." And so Manohar was packed off to Sholapur.

Sulking, Nilofar had shut herself in her room. That evening Ahmad bhai had bought naans and kebabs from Bhindi Bazaar, but Nilofar didn't open the door. By chance Ehsaan sahib also wandered in it the same time and seeing Ahmad bhai, tried to make a quick exit, but was waylaid.

Ahmad bhai was already in a bad mood, so in a very short while the two were at loggerheads – but not openly. The minute the Begum got up to leave the room for a few minutes, they started arguing:

"What's this mess you got me in, you rotten fellow? First the film goes down the drain and now ..."

"What's the matter seth? Did you visit Hakeemji again?"

"To hell with Hakeemji. He was also out to cheat me. You scoundrels, you're all thieves."

"Look, the girl needs only two things. If she gets both, then ..."

"What are you saying? I don't understand."

"If you want me be to be frank, well, then I'm saying give the girl love so that she'll be crazy for you, or shower her with clothes and jewellery."

"Did I not love her enough?" Ahmad bhai's voice cracked.

"Well for the last few months you've been quite stingy. The Begum is very worried. I hear she pawned some jewellery to Raghunath to get the money for the children's fees. It's not easy to get the jewellery back from Raghunath's clutches."

"Do you think I'm a fool? I give the girl money and then she kicks me?"

Just then the Begum returned from the bathroom and Ehsaan sahib began jabbering:

"Jawaharlal from the CPCI is offering seventy, but I told him I won't accept less than one lakh. Why take a picture unless one's demands are met? There's no dearth of distributors. In fact I'm thinking of starting my own distribution agency. I've talked to Surajmal about this and we've come to an agreement."

Ahmad bhai's blood was boiling. He knew very well, and the Begum did too, that Ehsaan sahib was making all this up and one wouldn't find enough money in his pocket for even two cups of tea. He had had a train pass made and had been showing it off to everyone. Every time he pulled out the handkerchief from his pocket the first-class pass fell out. He had very cleverly renewed the pass each month.

"Would you lend me fifteen rupees please?" he would ask. "The pass is about to expire."

The industry is so large that even a poor extra, to whom he had promised a running role in a film, would lend him fifteen rupees. It was hard to say anything about producers — they were mysterious beings. Today he would be penniless with nowhere to go and tomorrow he would meet someone who wanted to convert his black money to white, or come across an actor who would take pity on him and become a guarantor and in no time he would be on his feet again. Like a half-dead mouse, which jumps back to life after being made to sniff some food, Ehsaan sahib too needed the kind of help that seemingly arrives from nowhere. As a matter of fact, he had also died and been returned to life many times. If his wife had not run away he would not be in this situation today.

When the Begum went out again to get some tea, Ahmad bhai screamed again.

"What nonsense is this? I know everything. Surajmal is nothing but a crook. And I'm telling you upfront, it has nothing to do with money, the girl doesn't speak to me."

Ehsaan sahib laughed mockingly, making Ahmad bhai break into a sweat.

"You're a crook, you're trying to ..."

The Begum returned with the tea and Ehsaan sahib quickly said:

"All right, I have to leave now. I have an appointment with Abrar Alvi about the story." He spoke thoughtlessly. He had forgotten that just the day before he had mentioned a sitting with Bedi, and now the appointment was with Alvi. The Begum knew this, but she didn't think it was necessary to probe.

Just recently he had said to her:

"How would our Nilofar do in the role of a dancer?"

The Begum thought that if Nilofar succeeded in landing a role in a film then their troubles would be over. Already people in the industry had begun to think of mother and daughter as whores. Ever since Ahmad bhai had suspended his bounty and doled out money with the utmost reluctance, the Begum had started making trips to the studios.

"Well, all Baby wants is to work in your film. She doesn't care anything about money. Just the other day a man came with a message from Mehboob sahib. He wanted her to come and see him. It was for a running role. But she said, 'No, they have Kum Kum over there.' Now tell me, is Kum Kum a real dancer? You haven't seen Baby dance. You never come. Do come over to the house one day." The Begum would speak coquettishly and the poor inexperienced producer would be taken in, although he knew very well that the Begum was just trying to curry favour with him and that if he offered her daughter a role, she would begin making unreasonable demands.

Anyway, the unlucky producer was enticed with the "working for free" idea and began spending money on her. She was working for free, so what was the harm if the Begum's friends consumed five or six glasses of lassi and ate omelettes and toast, he thought.

People had begun to understand that the Begum was now trying to make Nilofar's lover jealous so that when Ahmad bhai came and Nilofar didn't want to see him, she could say:

"You know, Filmistan's production manager was here. In a Chevrolet. There's a party at Jalan Seth's." Or, "The art director of Prakash's colour film was here, he was going to take her to buy some saris of her choice."

Nilofar started working in many such films. Ahmad bhai was won over and the Begum fought with the producer and the work came to an end. How could she work for free while Ahmad bhai was still around?

But for how long could Ahmad bhai remain in business? His father-in-law had lost five lakhs at the races; years of earnings were depleted in one day. In the meantime, those who were about to declare him bankrupt began harassing him for money. Locks appeared on his Colaba and Bandra general stores and Nilofar's flat was also threatened.

The Begum lost her wits. The children were home for the holidays and the question of sending them back to school after the holidays didn't arise. The house was sunk in mourning. And Nilofar, playfully popping chocolates in her mouth, was laughing.

When the plush-covered furniture was about to be dragged out, the Begum hastily tied up all the jewellery in a corner of her sari's pallu and stuffed it inside her petticoat, all the while shouting at Nilofar. As fate would have it, the door on the western side of the flat opened, and Ehsaan sahib walked in with Surajmal, as if they had come from some void beyond.

Soon the price of the flat and the furniture was paid. The papers were placed in the Begum's lap and Surajmal didn't even look at Nilofar's supple calf, flashing through the blue nightgown like lightning in the clouds.

Surajmal Kanodia had not acquired his wealth recently. His great-great-grandfather had owned several general stores in Delhi. Perhaps it was he who had invented the art of mixing tiny white stones with rice. Mixing larger stones with dal has many advantages – it won't strain the housewife's eyes when she's picking out the stones, and there's no danger of their being left in as anyone with poor eyesight can also spot them. White wood shavings in flour act as a kind of vegetable; he imported this sawdust from Japan. You can't cause any harm if you blend about two ounces of suet to every two pounds of ghee; suet is also animal fat and is equally beneficial. It's advantageous to mix ground saffron flowers with turmeric; it has a cooling effect. There's no harm in removing the kernels from the coriander seeds and selling them separately, or taking out a few seeds from the cardamom pods. Actually he was a very saintly person. Many ashrams were supported by his donations.

Surajmal was a graduate. He was fashionable, his wife had an Intermediate degree, was an expert at singing and dancing, and was very beautiful, and they had four children. It was a life filled with love. But just to change the taste, he generally kept three or four girls on the side. It helped him in his business. He didn't like serving alcohol to friends at home, especially since prohibition. The real fun he had was with these girls and Nilofar had been part of his plan for a very long time. He wanted to maintain her in a very luxurious style. Ahmad bhai had been a stingy man, snivelling whenever he had to pay for something.

Surajmal wanted to invest in films, but the conditions under which he wanted to make that investment were not acceptable to the big-name producers. He wanted sixty per cent interest annually and payments in black had to be made to the artists and the music director as well. If the budget for a film was ten lakhs, of which two lakhs would go toward the interest, four for black money payments, all that remained was four lakhs and that's how much the film was to be made with. Presenting a four-lakh film as a ten-lakh project was an art that only two-bit producers could manage.

Ehsaan sahib was also one of these producers. After finding him, Surajmal was convinced that now the era of Mehboob, Shantaram and Bimal Roy was over. Now only Surajmal Film Productions would reign supreme.

He did not like Nilofar's flat in Dadar at all, so he bought a flat on A Road, Churchgate, and transferred the entire family there. But Surajmal was not like Ahmad bhai. He was put off by Nilofar's cheap behaviour and he had not even felt the desire to touch her. He wanted to give her some leeway. Sometimes he would pinch her cheek, or pat her on the hip. He wasn't ready yet to assign her a higher status than this. She was also a little uncouth. After having stayed so long in Ahmad bhai's company she had acquired a certain coarseness and frequently used the abusive Bombay dialect. She would leer like a gangster, as if saying, "You won't do it my way? Well, shall I become naked then?"

But Surajmal was not affected by her nakedness in the least, or maybe he didn't show that he was. What he really liked about her was her respectable lineage. He had enjoyed all the cultures of Hindustan. He was looking for a woman with special qualities, the kind he had come across in the grand brothels of Delhi, Agra, and Banaras. He spoke excellent Urdu and became upset when he heard the Bombay dialect.

In the beginning Nilofar felt revulsion, but then she began to tolerate him and finally she began to like him. She put on her respectable persona to make him happy. She started dressing modestly. Once or twice she surprised him in her dressing gown and somewhat agitated, he left the room quickly. After this she started getting ready properly before he came.

He began taking her out with him openly. In his company she attended lively, fun-filled parties, picnics, musical programmes, and clubs, although she was aware that there were three other girls like herself. She knew that these girls had children by the seth; but they all had comfortable lives. Their children went to English-medium schools and in their respective neighbourhoods they themselves were regarded as the seth's wives. The seth did not believe in making any kind of a fuss; he came quietly to visit, stayed for a while and then left. Sometimes his friends also visited and occasionally, if he deemed it fit, he would lend his mistress to a friend. If the friend so desired, he would even give her up altogether; he would sell her along with the flat and the children.

The question arose, how did he manage to take care of all these families? The details are very long and convoluted, but they may be helpful to understand his style of operation.

The seth used the names of these girls as a front for business. The girls didn't have enough sense or intelligence to understand or suspect anything. They signed whatever papers he asked them to sign, and they didn't know that they were engaged in deals involving lakhs of rupees. Contracts were issued in their names, all within the limits of the law. Whatever was saved in income tax and super taxes was more than was required for their expenses.

Since Nilofar was educated, she realised that the money being issued out to Ehsaan sahib was in her name and that she was the owner of the company. If she decided to be dishonest, the seth would have no recourse.

Realising the extent of her own power, she felt special. When she explained the situation to the Begum, she too was overjoyed, but what was the use of creating trouble? He was a decent man, and it was all for their own good, there was no dearth of anything. The Begum was sensible.

Gradually she arranged it so that Nilofar was referred to as Rani sahiba. The seth couldn't help smiling. All his women were queens in their own neighbourhoods, but they didn't know each other and each thought of herself as a queen.

When by God's grace, Nilofar became pregnant the seth was overly excited; it would seem he had received news that a eunuch had delivered a son. He took her to the doctor himself, gave her vitamins and tonics with his own hand and constantly instructed her to be careful.

But on the day of the opening ceremony of his film, he took his wife to sit next to him during the puja. Nilofar wasn't feeling well, but she insisted she was going too and at the puja was adamant that she would sit with him.

"I'm the real producer, the puja will be with me sitting next to him."

"The money is the seth's, go along with what he has decided," Ehsaan sahib explained.

"Look here, what's this silliness," the Begum also scolded.

When pictures were being taken, she plonked herself next to him, but at the last minute Ehsaan sahib would appear between her and the seth. She would try to get into the middle in every picture that was being taken, but after a slight rearrangement she would always find herself in a corner.

When the pictures appeared in the newspapers, her name casually showed up somewhere with the names of the extras who were also at the opening. When, as she was accustomed to doing, she tried to quarrel with the seth the next day, he first gave her a spoonful of tonic and then gently explained: "This has to with business, women shouldn't meddle needlessly. You'll gradually understand and then you won't talk such nonsense."

But Nilofar had become a queen. She wasn't satisfied. No matter how unwell she was, she would go to the shooting and she would criticise every little thing.

"Why is so much time being wasted?"

"The production manager is a thief."

"This song is not fast enough, it's not lively."

"Why does this heroine demand black? Why does the hero arrive at two? Everyone is lazy, no one wants to work."

The Begum agreed with everything she said and the two of them bickered with everyone. People didn't say anything in front of them, but behind their backs they called them names.

When Nilofar gave birth to an unattractive girl the Seth was extremely disappointed. All his other mistresses had delivered boys first. His wife also had three sons and one girl for whom he would easily find a bridegroom for a few lakhs, although she was uglier than Nilofar's daughter.

He became a little disenchanted after the girl's birth. He was also busy with work. Then a rumour surfaced that a very stunning girl had arrived from the Punjab and he was being seen everywhere with her. When Nilofar tried to quarrel with the seth he laughingly hedged:

"Oh, the poor girl is looking for work. I told Ehsaan sahib to give her some small role."

"But the picture is complete. What small role?" the Begum asked.

"There was a dance number in a café that was still needed," Ehsaan sahib said.

"But you said nothing more was needed."

"The distributor asked for one more dance," said the seth.

"Why don't you understand? You start arguing without thinking." Ehsaan sahib spoke angrily.

"And you understand everything? Be quiet. Don't make me say more. You pimp for prostitutes and put on airs?"

"Look, let it be, what's the use of saying all this?' the seth said gently.

"Why should I let it be?"

"Ehsaan sahib, why don't you stay quiet."

"I'm quiet sethji. One can only damage one's own honour by talking to these bitches."

"Your mother must be a bitch." Nilofar lost control. The same Nilofar whose Bismillah was celebrated when she was four, who used to sing with a lisp, "*lab pe aati hai dua ...*" and Dadi Bi would recite the prayer to keep her safe from the evil eye, who knew the seven *kalimas,* who when she read the salaam made listeners weep – that same Nilofar was now behaving worse than the washer-women in uttering filthy oaths.

Ehsaan sahib was no less skilful. His expletives were expansive and deep. But the seth just sat smiling through all this. And he continued smiling until Nilofar picked up a high-heeled shoe and hit Ehsaan sahib so forcefully that he suffered a nosebleed. He threatened to call the police, but the seth succeeded in pacifying him. After this incident the seth didn't visit for many days. Nilofar called several times, and each time she was told he was asleep, or not at home, and when she persisted, the phone went dead. But she didn't have any monetary problems. Money covering the month's expenses arrived on the twenty-eighth in the form of a cheque. For the first time she actually noted that the receipt was for the amount she had received. All the money she had been given until now had been delivered in the same way. If the seth wanted he could take back this money. It was for the film. In addition to this who knows how many other receipts she had signed. She had also signed some blank papers. It's true that the flat was hers, and in addition the jewellery must be worth one lakh rupees or perhaps even one and a half lakhs. The Begum panicked. For no reason at all they had disturbed a hornet's nest.

Nilofar refused to sign the receipt. The seth said nothing. But on the fourth day the cheque was returned by the bank.

No one in the peaceful atmosphere of A Road heard the curses and foul language that passed between the Begum and Nilofar during their battle, nor could anyone hear the sound of the shoes they pounded each other's heads with, nor did anyone see them when they put their arms around each other and made up after all the weeping and shouting.

The Begum went straight to Ehsaan sahib and fell at his feet. He had also been quite concerned and they quickly made up. Then they both went to see the seth. He never saw anyone at home in connection with business so they had to wait for several hours in the office. Just like a seasoned madam representing high-class courtesans, she assured the seth that Nilofar was despondent without him, she hadn't stopped crying, and if he didn't come to see her, she would kill herself.

The seth was all sweetness and immediately said, "I've been very busy. The picture has to be delivered. You can ask Ehsaan sahib, I haven't had time even to breathe. The Madras distributor is harassing us, he keeps complaining that we've delayed the delivery." And then he began giving them the details of his business-related problems.

Just then that fresh new bud from the Punjab came in, looking shy and bashful. There was a film premiere to go to. Nilofar had been yearning to go to this premiere for a long time and had already bought a new sari for the occasion. The seth stood up quickly and went to the adjoining room with her. The Begum waited in vain. Finally it was discovered that he had quietly slipped away.

"Didn't I say the seth is a bastard? If he makes up his mind about something, nobody can change it. Nilofar no longer has the same appeal as she had before."

"What do you mean?" The Begum pretended to be startled. Not only the Begum, but Nilofar as well had been afraid of this. Seth Surajmal had never been mad about her like Ahmad bhai, although he had spent two years with her.

If Nilofar hadn't been so stubborn she could have stayed with him forever. He had never left anyone in the lurch, but she had insulted him by refusing to sign the receipt and he couldn't tolerate anyone doubting his intentions. But he had forgiven Nilofar.

When Nilofar saw Ehsaan sahib's face she looked at him angrily. Her blood was boiling. She was angry at the whole world, and she vented that anger on her little girl also.

"Send this wretched creature to him also."

"God knows what she's planning now." Ehsaan sahib became irritated.

"Why? Why should I raise this bastard girl?"

"Don't be crazy."

"Wait and see, I'll make them all sweat. Does he think I'm the child of a merchant?"

"Nilofar bibi – you're out to snatch sugarcane from an elephant. Do you think the seth is an idiot? What are you thinking?"

"But the girl is the seth's daughter, isn't she? Does she not have any rights?" The Begum asked.

"Whether the girl is his or not is not a matter for discussion, but she has no special privileges because legally she's not his daughter. None of the seth's mistresses' children have any share in his wealth."

"What do you mean?"

"I mean you're a fool. What name were you admitted with in the hospital?"

"Hospital? I don't know. But all the bills were paid by sethji."

"Yes, but the child's father's name?"

"It must be sethji's name. What other name could it be?"

"No, that's where you're mistaken."

"So, whose name is it?"

"Well, let it go, what's the use of talking about all this."

"Why don't you tell me?"

"Look, I'm scared of you. Your hands aren't under control, and neither is your tongue."

"No, no, don't worry. Tell me."

"The name is mine."

"Yours? Have you gone mad?"

"All right, tell me then, what should I have done? Should I have refused? Look Nilofar, this squabbling won't help any of us," he said, when he saw blood rising in Nilofar's eyes. "Listen with a cool head or I'm off," he threatened.

After a reasonable exchange of curses and foul language, he said:

"If you want to talk about rights, then legally you are my wife. The seth didn't want to get into this predicament from the beginning. He had brought you here with the promise that I carry out a nikah with you and ..."

"Oh you wretch, have you lost your mind? How could you have had a nikah? A one-sided nikah?"

"It was a regular nikah. I have a nikahnama to prove it."

"What? Nikahnama? How did that happen?"

He grabbed Nilofar's hand. After raining curses on him, she had now resorted to hitting him with shoes.

"A fake nikahnama!" the Begum said. "Are you planning to spend time in jail?"

"Begum, I'm not an idiot. And I swear, my intentions are entirely honest. You should be grateful to me that your granddaughter is not illegitimate and the seth is also happy. I swear by God, I only did this because I thought, after all she's a respectable girl, if she has children she won't be able to show her face."

The Begum didn't understand. Because she had become so thick-skinned she had lost even the ability to be surprised. Still, she asked:

"But how did this fake nikah take place?"

"Doesn't matter how it happened. There is a signature."

"What signature?"

"Your daughter's, and then the signatures of two witnesses."

"Who knows how those signatures were obtained. God knows how many other things will appear with her signatures. Do we have the flat or is that gone with the signatures too? So many times I said, 'you foolish girl, you're educated, look before you sign'. She just closed her eyes and signed her death sentence."

"Yes, the flat is still yours, but I can't say what will happen in the future. If Nilofar behaves coolly and wisely then ..."

"What will happen now?" the Begum said, rubbing her palms sorrowfully.

"So you're now my husband?" Nilofar guffawed.

"Nilofar, what is this insolence?" The Begum was angry. Perhaps because of their old association she still harboured some regard for Ehsaan sahib.

"Oh, I'm talking to my husband."

"That's enough. If you continue with any more rubbish I'll hit you with a shoe."

"How much is the mehr, my dear husband?"

"The usual sharia mehr, thirty-two rupees."

"Cash." Nilofar bellowed another laugh. The lively inhabitants of A Road thought how cheerful she was, this queen of laughter! The bhajans had started in the temple downstairs. The intoxicating fragrance of all the items for puja was filling the air. The chime of the harmonium combined with the beat of the drum and the tinkling of small cymbals had livened up the atmosphere. The pujari was singing a film song in a voice that resembled the vibrations of a broken flute:

"*Devta, I have your support, I'm clinging to the edge of your garment.*" Or perhaps: "*You are clinging to the edge of my garment.*" Whatever fits well in a film song is what's right. No one here knows what is yours, what is mine. Is God clinging to man's garment or is man clinging to God's garment? It makes no difference. The way the pujari is singing it seemed as if man and God were at each other's throats. Nilofar was laughing hysterically. How strange indeed the sport that God plays. Her mother's lover was her husband! Law and husband, husband and law – all are rocks on the side of a road used to crush the skulls of girls like Nilofar. That was why there were flames raging in her laughter. And far away, in the dreamy atmosphere of Juhu, a fresh new bud of the Punjab was slowly, gradually, becoming a flower. The embers of lust were crackling in the seth's eyes. Tomorrow was the opening of Shagufa's first film. She was the heroine and was investing her own money. Her money – the seth's money – her body – and the seth's body!

This is love – and this is business.

FOUR

"BUT WHEN DID THIS GODDAMN nikah take place? Where?" asked the Begum.

"In Lakheempur. Before coming to this flat."

"Look here my dear man, show some sense. I should have you arrested."

"Yes, if you take the matter to court you might win. But why do that? If you want I can give a divorce today. I did this for your welfare."

"To hell with my welfare. Give her a divorce."

"Think coolly about this." Ehsaan sahib smiled.

"Think about what?"

"It's possible sethji will come around. Although he never takes back what he has got rid of. Look, I helped as much as I could. What more can I do? But don't worry. The children's fees will arrive on time, and the expenses for the house will be met."

"But why didn't he come? You should have told him that Nilofar misses him very much." Nilofar's voice cracked.

Ehsaan sahib broke into a laugh.

"You talk like a child. He's a temperamental man, our

sethji. If he develops a soft spot for someone then it's great, but if he turns away, then ..."

"May God forgive us, what crime did the girl commit?" the Begum asked.

"It was a deal involving the heart."

"Huh! The bastard with a heart!" Nilofar screamed.

"Listen, what's the use of all this nonsense? The snake has escaped and you're still sitting there rubbing the mark it left behind."

"If I don't crush the head of the snake you can call me a harlot, not Nilofar."

"Why are you upsetting yourself?" Ehsaan sahib patted her hand.

"May you die!" Nilofar violently pushed his hand away.

"What's this? I may not even touch you?"

"No."

"And why my dear?"

"I feel nauseated."

"Allah, what conceit! The rope is burnt but the knot is still there. This haughtiness won't do now, Miss sahib. Gone are the days when Khalil Khan flew pigeons. You've been in this profession for ten years, right?"

"Yes, so what?"

"At thirty a woman starts sagging."

"Look here, why are you making things up? Who is thirty?" The Begum intervened. "Come on girl, go to your room. This wretch is bent on saying whatever rubbish comes into his head."

"I've sagged, this is what he's saying, isn't he?" said Nilofar with a venomous look.

"I'm saying it, time is saying it, and if that weren't the case, sethji would be sitting at your feet instead of being with Shagufa."

"So I'm old now, is that what you mean?"

"I didn't say that, but you're not so new and fresh either."

"I have sagged?" She ripped off her blouse with both hands and stood taut before him. "Look, you blind man."

He stared aghast at the raging storm before him. The plate slipped from the Begum's hands.

"Hai, hai, you stupid girl! Have you gone mad? Aren't you ashamed?"

"No, I'm not ashamed." Nilofar laughed loudly and tearfully and, pushing back her hair in one swift motion, she came and stood right in front of Ehsaan sahib.

"Look bastard, I have sagged. So why has your manliness died, you fool?"

Ehsaan sahib laughed apprehensively and wiped the sweat from his forehead with his sleeve.

"Go and change your clothes." The Begum pulled her by the arm.

"No, I won't." Nilofar forced her hand away.

"The lecherous scoundrels in the flat across the street are watching you."

"Let them watch. Look here, if you make me angry I'll go out just like this." She turned toward the balcony.

But before she could go out the Begum began protesting hotly. She started calling Ehsaan sahib names. He immediately grabbed Nilofar and threw her on the sofa.

And then ensued a pitched battle in which Ehsaan sahib, the Begum, the cook and ayah were on one side, and on the other a half-naked Nilofar was turning them all to pulp.

Whatever was breakable she shattered to bits, and then she started picking up things to throw down from the balcony.

And just then, as if by magic, Surajmal Kanodia entered the room. For a few minutes he just looked at the mêlée, smiling.

"Leave her alone," he said, slowly pushing Ehsaan sahib out of the way. An enchanting heat began smouldering in his eyes. He appeased the flaming, fiery Nilofar in one minute. The Nilofar who was accustomed to acting arrogantly, who used to make Ahmad bhai pick up her shoes with his teeth and massage her feet, that same Nilofar now dropped into Surajmal's embrace like a kite cut off from its string.

Wantonness was now in her blood. For ten years the object of her existence had been the worship of pleasure. A few days of coldness on the part of the seth had turned her life upside down. Sethji was involved with a new girl, so had her body indeed sagged? No – she couldn't even imagine such a horrifying thing. Her pride suffered at the thought. Her body was her only asset. Without it she had no identity – she didn't exist. Much crying and temper tantrums ensued. The seth kissed every part of her body and swore devotion. There was fire blazing in him as well. The other girl had been acquired merely to tease Nilofar. She turned out to be a nasty person and he regretted taking her to the movies.

That night was like her wedding night. The seth sent for his suitcase from the car parked downstairs and heaped bejewelled ornaments on her. Standing naked before him, piled from head to toe with jewellery, she blossomed in his hands.

"All right, put on your clothes and get ready," he said as he took the glass away from her lips and lovingly patted her hip.

"Why?"

"We'll go somewhere."

"Where?"

"Wherever we want. Get up."

Assembling all her arrows and her quivers, smiling shamelessly, she rose like a sword out of its sheath and ran to the bathroom.

"No wait, listen."

"What is it?" she asked coquettishly. Resting both her

hands on the door-frame, she turned to look at him. Today she had decided to sacrifice everything. The expertise of a young woman was something special after all.

"The business overseas came through."

"Really?" She came forward and sat on his knee.

"Yes. We made one lakh, five thousand rupees, of which thirty-five thousand is black."

"That's ours."

"Everything is yours, but ... but we have to make up for quite a lot of black. Go and get ready quickly. But first sign this document so that we can get the advance."

"A kiss first."

Sethji took a large mouthful of neat whisky, placed her head against his shoulder and then spat the whisky out over her face.

While she was signing, the seth had documents in one hand and a message of love in the other.

She came out dressed in a black sari and glittering jewels, her eyes shining with the gleam of the skies, her steps unsteady. She cast a glance at poor, scared Ehsaan sahib, then looked at her mother feeding her granddaughter. She was struck by a desire to snatch the child from her and never allow her to touch her again. She was going to show them both. Today she would ask the seth to get her a separate flat where she would live in peace with her beloved child. Now if only the seth's wife would die then she would have no more complaints.

That night was Nilofar's wedding night in the real sense of the word. How beautiful it was! Sethji had become young again. Even at the age of fifty-five his every move was filled with a special desire. Ahmad bhai had been a punishment, Manohar a foolishness. As for sethji, he seemed to know another way to fan a fire.

Then she could remember nothing. Where was she? Where was she flying?

She awoke to find the world swimming before her eyes. When her vision finally cleared she saw that she was in a strange room. Her black sari, which had shone like the expansive night sky was lying coiled up like a cobra in the middle of the room. There was no jewellery on her person. Her heart stopped for a moment. But then she broke into a smile at her foolishness. Sethji must have taken off her jewellery piece by piece. If only she hadn't been so intoxicated and had not been deprived of the pleasure of every single touch of his hand. But she couldn't even see any luggage or anything else. Perhaps things were in the other room, perhaps sethji was bathing. But a few moments of observation revealed that there was no other room. This was a single room. She started feeling nervous. There was a knock on the door and the bearer came in with a tray of tea. She quickly pulled the sheet over herself.

"Where is sahib?"

"Which sahib? No sahib came here."

"What nonsense is this you idiot."

"It's the truth begum sahib. Your driver brought you. It was very late, and only when he paid double did the manager agree to give you a room. The driver said you were sick." The bearer smiled meaningfully. He knew that the stuff under the blanket was quite good.

Nilofar's heart was beating violently. No, no, how could this be? Her heart was foolish and easily swayed. Did the sethji send her here alone? So who was the person who last night ... She tried to remember. There was definitely someone with her. There was an impression of a head on the pillow next to hers.

So someone had definitely been there. If not the seth, then who? Who took off her clothes and her jewellery? Her hair stood on end. Who was that ghost who made love to her in the darkness of the night and then disappeared? What if he had quietly strangled her?

But later when the manager in his office confirmed everything the bearer had told her, she put her head on the counter and burst into tears.

"The hotel bill has been paid. Why are you so worried? Perhaps because you were very sick and you can't remember anything. You must have come alone." He tried to sound sympathetic.

She felt like scratching the dog's face, but restraint had become a habit with her. She had become accustomed to tolerating Ahmed bhai's pyorrhoea-stricken breath, she had begun to recognise a whiff of fragrance in Surajmalji's burps, so why should it be difficult for her to tolerate the manager's devious comments?

"All right, please send for a taxi for me ..." She realised she didn't have a penny on her.

"The train has already left. Won't you go to the races in the evening?" He displayed his slimy smile again.

"No, I'll go home now, A Road, Churchgate."

"Madam, it will be difficult to go to Bombay in a taxi. If you stay until the evening, I'll take you there myself in my Chrysler."

"Why don't you call the taxi?"

"But it's possible we may not be able to easily get a taxi for Bombay today."

"What is this 'Bombay, Bombay' nonsense?"

"I mean a taxi to take you from Poona to Bombay."

"Poona?"

"Yes. This is the Poona Hotel. Didn't you read the sign? Perhaps last night you were quite ... I mean you were not feeling well at all." He smiled broadly again.

"Oh yes, I wasn't well" she lied. "So did sethji get a phone call?"

She cried silently and prayed: if only sethji had received a call from his home in the middle of the night informing him that his wife had died of heart failure. And because she had looked so peaceful when asleep sethji had not awakened her. Instead he had silently kissed her and slipped away.

"Which seth?"

"Kanodia seth."

"Who? Raghumalji or Tejmalji? Only last week Bhanmalji was here. He was having a roaring love affair with Shakuntala Bai at one time. She was mad about the Bade Seth Rongta and ..."

"I'm talking about Surajmalji." Nilofar became irritated. These bastards, how many seths are there? Fathers, sons, grandsons – all are suffering from the same addiction.

"Surajmalji?"

"Yes."

"What about him?"

"What do you mean? He came with me last night!"

"Madam, no seth came with you. You were alone. Perhaps the taxi driver carried you upstairs to your room."

Taxi driver! Her head began to spin like a top.

No, no, it was sethji. He was the one who had scooped her up in his arms and brought her up. It was him. She remembered the odour of his burp. When he put her down on the bed she had caught his shirt with her teeth. She remembered very well that he had stretched out on the floor right then.

But "he" wasn't wearing diamond buttons! Then it was the taxi driver. All at once her legs started trembling and she felt dizzy and fell into the big armchair in the corner.

"Madam!" The manager leapt toward her. "Come, let's go to your room."

"I have to make a call," she said after breakfast to the bearer who had come to clear up.

"Of course, of course," said the manager, who had been standing outside the door. He came in smiling. Nilofar was irked by his presence. How much he smiles, the damn fool, even his jaws don't tire from all this smiling.

"My purse fell from the car. I told the seth to stop the car but he said, 'Don't worry about it.' I said, 'There's seven hundred rupees in it,' and he said, 'Forget it, it's all right.'" She began weaving a web of lies. "Then he received a telegram saying his wife had been taken seriously ill."

She said this even though she knew that the wives of these seths neither get taken seriously ill nor do they ever die. But mistresses dream about such possibilities to comfort themselves. And the wives probably also entertain sweet dreams about the deaths of their husbands' mistresses. In truth, there is no damage to either the wives or the mistresses. The wives don't die and the mistresses keep coming. The first mistresses are still alive when the new ones appear, like new automobile models that arrive every year. There is no dearth of new goods.

"But what's the need for a trunk call? This hotel is also yours." The manager spoke in a voice dripping with emotion.

Nilofar had no energy left even to be startled or surprised. She was actually not looking forward to the trunk call herself. Amma would shower her with questions, start criticising every little thing: she would complain about the house rent and the children's fees and wouldn't send her a single penny. She knew there were still a few blank cheques left in her cheque book which could be cashed anywhere, in any "bank".

The manager couldn't be poor.

"So we'll go to the races in the evening?" the manager asked, his eyes brimming with anticipation.

"My clothes ..." she whined.

"Don't worry about clothes," he said almost choking with joy.

She sat in the Chrysler and they went shopping. She bought a couple of pairs of drainpipe trousers, some T-shirts, a dressing gown, and cosmetics. She also bought three or four saris and gave the blouses to a tailor for stitching. These were ready in an hour.

At the racecourse she encountered more of the manager's girlfriends than horses. He was anxious to start gambling as soon as possible. She also ran into several acquaintances from Bombay who had come to play at the races.

"Is seth sahib well?" some of them asked her as a mere formality.

"Yes, he is well," she replied casually. She was sure none of these people knew whether she was associated with a seth these days or not, but perhaps the story that she was the plaything of seths now written all over her face. The manager walked haughtily by her side, as if proud of the fact that he could temporarily buy the mistresses of rich men like one can buy second hand cars. Today the manager's luck was riding high. Whatever money he touched to Nilofar's lips before betting on a horse came back multiplied several times. And when Nilofar would touch him with her lips, then he too would be multiplied many times over. He had paid Nilofar her commission right there. But she didn't have a purse so the manager held on to her share. He was feeling very loving toward her. She was not only his beloved and his good luck charm, she had also lighted up his destiny.

The horses were running, the jockeys fastened to their backs like monkeys. The eyes of the crowds were fixed on red, yellow, purple and blue monkeys. There were tiny whips in their hands and the heels of their boots dug into the horses' sensitive thigh muscles. Women in vibrant-hued saris waved up and down and bucked the horses. An extremely fair Parsi lady, as large as an elephant, hopped energetically and practically pounded the tall man standing next to her. But he was unaware of it. He too was jumping on his seat as if he was a jockey atop a camel rather than a horse. A husband and wife began quarrelling after the race was over – they must be married since they were blaming each other for their respective defeats.

Race horses are fed morsels of gold as long as they are running, but when they are old they are shot and killed. Suddenly Ehsaan sahib's words echoed in Nilofar's ears. Was she getting old? For how long would she remain young? It had already been ten years. She broke into a sweat as she thought of the next ten years. What would she do after that? Thanks to seth Surajmal, her daughter was extremely plain in appearance and would never be a racehorse. A horse to be harnessed in a tonga or an ekka perhaps, but that was it. So what would the next ten years bring for her? The manager after the seth ... and then? How many more steps were there to climb down? And what would there be after the last step? Solid earth or a void?

She felt that her heart was breaking. The jockey's weight seemed to have been transported to her shoulders. The heels of the heavy boots dug into her womb, the whip cracked across her brain. The jockey, her mother, Ahmed bhai, Ehsaan sahib, sethji, the whole world weighed upon her!

"Let's go." She stood up that very instant.

"But the real race hasn't started yet."

"I don't care. I'm leaving."

"But listen. This is the last race. I've bet money on it, how can I just leave it and go? It's only a matter of five minutes."

Nilofar had never openly plied the prostitute's trade. She had regarded Surajmal almost as her husband and had begun to think of herself as a housewife; she still had some pride left. To her it appeared the manager was the lowest step of all. She had imagined the taxi driver to be sethji, so her conscience was clear. She was comforted by the thought that he was not the taxi driver but an unknown and mysterious person. She tried to think hard but couldn't remember how she came to be in the taxi. She had been in the seth's car. Had the seth just abandoned her to the care of a taxi driver and left? There was something mysterious about all this. How could this have happened? And then her heart broke again when she thought: why couldn't it have happened? Everything is possible. Masooma can become Nilofar, her mother can become a madam, her father could forget everyone, her brothers could turn away from her. So why should the seth have acted as if he were related to her?'

She drank so much alcohol in order to digest the manager that even if she had had to sleep with a dog she would have been able to kiss it fervently. That day she took long strides towards the lowest point of depravity. Naked, she romped around the room, then she jumped into the bathtub filled with hot water. Rejecting the manager's advances, she continued her wild behaviour in the tub. With great difficulty he got her out. Seated on the floor, leaning her head against the commode, she suddenly burst into tears. Her intoxication began to wear off. The manager became fearful.

"You want to rob my honour you rotten wretch! Bastard!" She started picking up the things in the bathroom to throw at him.

The poor manager was bewildered and sitting down on the chair he began wiping the sweat off his face with his handkerchief. That was when she felt great pity for him. One day she had seen a crippled dog at Chowpatti. Crawling inside his open wounds were maggots that looked like white grains of rice. Nilofar had broken into sobs when she saw the dog. She felt nauseated at the sight of the manager's bulging eyes, but she reminded herself of the injured dog and clucked.

"Come here, come ... Moti, Moti ..."

Looking apprehensive, a pitiable look spreading on his face, he slowly inched forward towards her. Cautiously he took a towel and rubbed her dry. She remained silent. Then he quietly helped her to bed and covered her with a blanket. Nilofar started laughing. Fearful of the waning intoxication, she quickly gulped down another glassful and kicked the blanket off. The manager felt himself crumpling. Holding back the vomit of white crawling rice heaving in her throat, she stretched her arms toward him.

In three days she drank more than she had done in all her life. She discovered that the manager was not such a difficult morsel to swallow after all. She had forgotten to buy a purse, but the poor fellow had been giving her more money than she had earned. Well, I'll collect everything when I'm ready to leave, she thought. She didn't really know how to take care of money and only carried a purse because it was fashionable to do so. For years she had not looked at money properly. Like a coin-minting machine she made money that was then efficiently managed by her mother. She had read in books: "a mother suffers all the sorrows in the world for her children, she grinds wheat and she sews clothes to keep her children fed." But not only had her mother never ground grain on a millstone, she had never even tried to grind sandalwood. Her maternal grandmother had raised her, her aunts had always knitted sweaters and stitched frocks for her, teachers had taught her. Yes, it's true her mother kept each child in her belly for nine months. If she could help it perhaps she might have had a nanny or a midwife carry her children instead for nine months. And now she was receiving the payment for those nine months from Nilofar, along with interest.

Now she started praying for her mother's death. It would be so amusing to see her swollen face wrapped in a white shroud. Then she would have a strong, cemented grave built for her and make sure there was incense burning on it all the time. Then demands made for the children's fees would cease. Why was she caring for her mother's children anyway?

She was also her mother's daughter. Why did she make demands on her as if she were her husband?

She slept all day. In the afternoon she would go for a ride in the Chrysler. On returning around six in the evening the drinking would start. A session filled with pleasure would stretch late into the night. On the fourth day it seemed to her as though she had been living with the manager for years and she was now tired of him. How drawn out the days, how long the nights, like the devil's intestines, the dreams so tangled and incomplete!

When she was bored, she called the manager names and threw shoes at him. Then when he gazed at her with the look of the half-dead crippled dog she giggled and clung to him. Bored with the same old thing, she decided she would go back to Bombay. The manager became apprehensive. He showed her French films to amuse her. She actually threw up when she saw them and spat on his face. One day, shutting herself in the bathroom, she sat on the floor and resting her head against the commode, cried for hours until there was no water left in her eyes – it was as if the spring from where her tears originated had dried up.

"What is this foolishness?" she asked herself finally and, her spirits dampened, she returned to lie down on her bed. She had a headache and her heart was raging with frightening storms. Suddenly she sat up in bed. Darkness had crawled into the room. The manager was shouting at the servants. The hotel guests were shut up in their rooms doing who knows what. The bottle in the cupboard yielded enough for only one drink. Irked, she rang the bell for the bearer.

"Bring me a taxi. I want to go to Bombay."

"The train doesn't go to Bombay at this time."

Oh! When was the train of her fate destined to leave? She became anxious and fretful. When the manager showed up she made obscene remarks and laughed. Then she insisted on seeing the same French film that had earlier made her vomit.

That day the manager had been drunk. Today he was in control.

"If someone reports this, my hotel will be in trouble," he said, making excuses. "Last year someone reported it to the police and I was shut down. Luckily Nawab sahib intervened and told them it was one of his films and I was let off the hook."

"And then?"

"What then? I greased their palms."

"And then?"

"Well, the bastards themselves started watching the film."

When Nilofar saw the film again she became agitated.

"Why do they watch these films? May they die, these wretched men!"

"For pleasure, and secondly ..."

"And secondly what?"

The manager smiled at her.

"Let's not talk about it."

"Come on, tell me."

"Isn't Surajmalji fond of this?"

"Of what?"

"Don't act so innocent."

The manager told her that many of the guests staying in the hotel had strange tastes. "When men get tired after taking care of business in Bombay they come here to relax. If a hotel doesn't provide girls and alcohol, it won't last long."

"Where do they get the girls from?"

"Well, we don't even have to supply the girls. The girls come by themselves or their pimps give us commission so they can be made available to the seths. Some of the guests make arrangements before they come. I don't supply anything myself. The bearers take care of everything. I just look the other way."

"Some day you'll be caught."

"Well, we're not inexperienced fools, you know. Unless the matter is fixed firmly, my bearers won't even touch it. The register is always up to date and we have to bribe officials as well."

"And why is that?"

"So that they don't bother us. Even if we don't conduct any illegal business, we still have to deal with many problems. They keep pestering us if we don't hand out bribes. The head bearer also used to become troublesome. The rascal started agitating about forming a union. I explained that my employees never wanted for anything and could eat as much as they wished. True, there's a six per cent share for the management in the tip, but that's a tiny amount. But the bastard started sprouting wings. He had been with me for eight years and never had a single complaint. Suddenly who knows what came into his head, he started saying all kinds of stupid things. He had some scoundrels on his side, about three or four, and I fired them all. And do you know – they started a sit-in right in front of the hotel and made everyone's life miserable. The guests were really inconvenienced. But I took care of them, showed them a thing or two."

"Oh! How?" Nilofar was enjoying the manager's bragging.

"I had a whole case of foreign liquor planted in the bastard's house and sent the police after him."

"Oh my!"

"So what if I spent about a thousand or so, at least the entire staff was happy."

"Why?"

"Well, only one bottle would have been enough as evidence in the court and we presented a dozen. The police brought the rest of the bottles here to this very hotel and had a great time drinking and carousing."

"How wicked you all are. And these anti-corruption people, don't they bring any of these men to task?" Nilofar was drinking herself, but she became angry at hearing this.

"What anti-corruption? Do you think we have ordinary guests? We have contacts with very important people. It's impossible that anything could go wrong. Yes, it's true though that first we had to deal with one and now it's two we have to consider."

"You mean corruption and anti-corruption?"

"Yes my dear."

That same night Nilofar's decency further plummeted.

Under the manager's tutelage she learned the arts shown in these French films, smoked her first dhatoora cigarette and also tested a morphine injection. After watching the films a few times, she began to enjoy them. Not only had her body been laid bare, her soul also became naked. This was the same Nilofar who had burst into tears when her aunt once walked into the bathroom while she was bathing. Her aunt had sworn that it was dark in the bathroom and she hadn't seen anything, but Nilofar had sensed her presence. But today her honour was dancing naked to the beat of evil spirits.

It was evening. Nilofar's body was aching and she was feeling very sleepy. She had not heard anything about her family since her arrival in Poona nor had she made an attempt to get in touch with them. Was her mother worried? The same mother who used to be reluctant to send her over to her aunt's house because she had grown-up sons. She had been gone for so many days but perhaps her mother didn't care now, as if Nilofar was not a real woman, but one whose virtue had been soiled. Well, what fear does the mother of a dishonourable woman have? She does not fear that someone might strangle her daughter, or hack her body and throw it into the river. She was no longer the symbol of honour for her mother, but was instead the bazaar's honour. Her honour had been severed at its very foundation.

Suddenly the manager ran in looking flustered.

"Something terrible has happened."

"What has happened?"

"Raja sahib is here. Surajmal's brother-in-law is a bastard."

"What are you talking about?" Nilofar asked irately. Who is this damn Raja sahib who has come? Why are you so jumpy?"

The manager looked uncomfortable. Then he said angrily: "The bastard says, 'Wake her up'. That mother f ..."

"I don't know what you're going on about. Wake up whom?"

"You," he said in a tearful voice.

"Look here, I am awake." If only she were not awake. If only this had been a dream, a dream she had been having for ten years, a burning dream of hell – and then she would wake up. Picking up her books she would say to Amma: "I have a history test today, if you want me to have breakfast, make it quickly, otherwise I'm off." But perhaps she hadn't really slept. Perhaps she had never slept, and the virginal sleep of her young days would never kiss her eyes again. Her eyes wide open, she would keep staring into the void until one day she would be dead. And then, buried under tonnes of earth, all her dreams would shatter and turn into white crawling worms.

Then the manager told her that Surajmal had handed her over to Raja sahib. Actually it wasn't that he had handed her over, it was just that he was going away to Singapore and Hong Kong with his wife and children. The family was going first and he was going to leave later, directly from Delhi, with Shagufa. And for now the film was at a standstill.

"Who the hell do they think they are to stop the film? I'll

show them all. And that stupid Shagufa, I'll have her thrown out. Everything is in my hands."

"That's your affair. What do we do about Raja sahib?"

"Nothing, you fool."

"He's come to get you," the manager moaned.

"Why has he come to get me, the dog?"

"Speak softly, please."

"Why should I speak softly? Am I in his employ?

"In a manner of speaking you are. He has given your mother money to cover a month's expenses."

"What?"

"Why don't you talk to him yourself."

"I have no desire to talk to him. You talk to him, refuse on my behalf."

"Refuse? But ..."

"Tell him we're getting married."

"Oh my God, what are you saying? He'll make life hell for me. Do you know, he's very friendly with extremely important and influential officials and ministers. It's easy to say that rajas and maharajas have ceased to exist but they are still around, and now have carefree lives, with no worries about estates or anything else. They get pocket money of fifteen lakh rupees and they have a grand life, the bastards. This hotel has been eyed for a long time. If I hadn't begged and explained that this was the source of my livelihood, he would have forced an advance on me and bought it by now. I have a five-year contract and it's about to expire. He's a real scoundrel."

"But I don't want to go with him."

"He ... he says to turn you out."

"Turn me out, he says? Is this his father's hotel? The dog!"

"It could be in fact. It is rumoured that Badi Rani sahiba had a special relationship with Mr Engineer."

"Who is Mr Engineer?"

"He was the uncle of this hotel's owner. He died childless. He left all his property to his nephew. Rani sahiba had given him a great deal."

"I see. Well, then turn me out."

"How can that be? No Nilofar bai." The manager's eyes filled again. "I begged and pleaded, the bastard started accusing me of trying to compete with the likes of him. 'Stay with your class of women', he said. He's crazy. Someone should tell that man that we're also human beings. What can we do if we fall in love?"

"So what will you do then?"

"That's what I'm asking. You tell me what to do."

"But I can't think of anything."

"How can I explain this to you ..."

The bearer knocked on the door.

"Raja sahib says it's getting late."

"Yes, yes, she's coming. She's taking a bath. Come on now, get ready quickly, get up." The manager adjusted the front of her dressing gown.

"No, I won't take a bath." Nilofar undid all her buttons. The manager became flustered. Instead of bringing the two sides of her dressing gown together, his sweaty hands began to wander.

"Listen," she said, wiping his drool from her neck.

"What?" Tears were flowing from the manager's eyes.

"Let's escape through the bathroom window and run away."

"No, we can't do that. He'll kill us." He was like a child who, scared off by the gardener, starts running but plucks flowers and crushes them as he runs, grabbing what he can – a whole flower or just a few petals.

"Why not?" Nilofar asked, pushing him away.

"Well ... the thing is that ... well, why don't you just get dressed."

"First tell me why not. Don't you like me?"

"Of course I like you."

"You're crazy about me?"

"Yes, I am."

"You can't live without me?"

"No I can't."

"All right then, let's elope."

"No ... but ..."

"Why? What are all these ifs and buts about?"

"Well, the thing is ... now how do I explain?"

"You've spent so much money on me, you have some rights over me too, don't you?"

"Well, that's what I'm saying. I'm in a terrible bind right now."

"Did he give you the full amount?" Nilofar asked, grasping the real situation at last.

"Yes," the manager said, looking up at the ceiling to avoid her gaze.

"And how much on top of that?"

"Not too much."

"How much? Tell me." She kicked him.

"Ten thousand." The manager moved out of her range.

"Then return it."

"Return it? He won't take it back."

"Go and throw it in his face. If you love me then return the money. Can't do it?"

"I'm helpless."

"You're helpless?"

"Yes, I'm a poor man, with a family. My employer harasses me all the time. I can open a small hotel with this money. I'll be rid of him forever this way."

"You're a family man?"

"Yes Nilofar bai."

"And you're crazy about me."

Silence!

"And you can't live without me?"

More silence!

"You can give your life for me but you can't give back the money?"

"But how will that help? He's very stubborn. How can I go against him?"

"All right then, kiss my lips once for the sake of the love you have for me."

The manager became excited.

"You won't have to spend anything. It will be free. Just this once. Come, take me in your arms." She dropped her dressing gown on the chair and stood up.

And when the manager's wet, drool-laden lips came close, she gathered together in her mouth all the anger and humiliation that was in her heart and spat on his face.

"Well done." Raja sahib was standing in the doorway, his eyes roving over her body. The manager made a hasty retreat.

"Actually the fault is all mine." He kicked the door shut and came and casually sat down on her bed with his back to her. "I had to preside over the annual mushaira and couldn't get away. I told them to get someone else, but they insisted that either I do it or else they would cancel the mushaira altogether. I thought since it was a fund-raiser for charity that I should go through with it. You know that when poets get together there's always a drinking programme that follows, and how could I not throw them a party? That's why I was busy for so many days."

Fastening the belt of her dressing gown, Nilofar came and sat down on the chair. She had seen Raja sahib at many parties and mushairas. He was sixty or sixty-five, but lean and solidly built. He was a pleasure seeker. Since he had lost his state many of the harem girls from his palaces were scattered here and there. Actually, not here and there; they had headed straight for the pleasure houses. Those who were more sophisticated had got married. Others were carrying on the same trade on a larger scale. In any case, Raja sahib's tastes had also changed. He had developed an interest in famous actresses and girls from good but ruined families. He was also very fond of musical events. Even though he was a raja, he was fully in tune with modern-day capitalism and was rapidly amassing a fortune in Bombay and other big cities; he had shares in many British firms, and was busily constructing flats in the posh Malabar Hill and Peddar Road and renting them on very high advances. He was revolted by Anglo-Indian and European women; in such matters he always favoured domestic goods over foreign goods. The home industry had benefitted greatly from this preference.

He had had his sights on Nilofar for a very long time but Surajmal had been standing in the way, because before Shagufa came along he had been genuinely fond of Nilofar. Raja sahib also liked one of Surajmal's mares, but he was not ready to sell her at any cost.

"Surajmalji, whenever you get tired of her, let me know," he would always say to him. Finally, he made Surajmal change his mind by making a very high offer; he got both the mare and Nilofar. The only problem was that he also had to purchase the film, which was under production, with its accompanying losses. This kind of buying and selling often takes place among friends and acquaintances. But he could make a profit on the film whenever he wished. The film was insured, the storage space was insured and any day there could be a fire and it would be possible to show double the loss incurred. The profit could therefore be converted into a loss. These are all skills related to business. He made so much profit in the Dadar textile mill that they couldn't handle it all. The very expensive machinery had been removed surreptitiously in the middle of the night and the mill had been set on fire. That same machinery was then shown to belong to someone else and bought at double the price. If anything went wrong, grand parties were thrown and old friendships came to the rescue. The problem was that when Raja sahib took over a company, it began spewing gold.

"But how did you buy that film? It's mine," Nilofar asked him when they were having dinner.

"It's the same film you sold to Surajmal."

"I didn't sell any film."

"I don't involve myself in any kind of risky business. My lawyer checked everything very carefully. You have signed bills of exchange for Surajmal."

"Bills of exchange? No, I didn't."

"You must have signed receipts."

"No. Yes, the children's fees were being sent, sometimes there were papers related to the studio, and the lawyer used to oversee everything."

"Your lawyer or Surajmal's?"

"My lawyer. Ehsaan sahib of course. Oh!" She was silenced suddenly.

"Ehsaan sahib? He's a real bastard."

"But we hadn't even quarrelled at that time."

"I don't understand what quarrels have to do with this. Surajmalji must have wanted to invest some money into his business in your name, but he's not a fool and he had to make sure his position was secure."

And people had said that Nilofar had trapped the seth, that she was amassing wealth with both hands.

"Oh well, forget him. He is a very clever man, a gullible girl like you fell into his hands and he had it made. You've just transferred the film to his name, you can't remember now."

And then Nilofar remembered: that day when the seth loaded her with jewels and worshipped at the altar of his lust, he had also managed to get her signature on some papers.

You stupid, dumb girl! She swore at herself. She felt the seth's hands crawling over her like scorpions and she shivered.

"Oh I see. You didn't realise what was happening. You know, this Kanodia is a fast worker. I'm flabbergasted when I hear stories of his exploits. He owns such a sprawling business, but has managed it so well that to this day he hasn't paid a penny in income tax. These income tax collectors make such a ceremony of procuring ten or fifteen rupees in taxes, but can never catch film artists who make lakhs in black. If the C.I.D. wants to apprehend him, I can suggest a hundred ways to do it. Actually his business uses innumerable names. He conducts much of his underhand activity in the name of all the girls he keeps."

"Or he does it in his wife's name."

"No. He's very honourable when it comes to his family. The only things in his wife's deposit box are jewels and gold."

Raja sahib was a frank and honest person. He made it very clear that this was a business relationship. He had never had a shortage of women, but for a long time he had been looking for a woman who could conduct herself like a society lady at high-class gatherings. He had to move in official circles and the "ladies" presently flourishing in Pavanpul and Colaba wouldn't do at all. She should be able to speak English but also be thoroughly cognisant with Hindustani culture. She could have a full, backcombed hairstyle, but should put her hands together in a namaste, or say aadaab arz like the women from the Lucknow nawab families. She should wear a handloom sari, but be able to delicately balance a cocktail in her hand. She should be a mixture that enchanted anyone who set eyes on her. In other words, for an ignorant Indian she should appear to be English, while an Englishman should regard her as a dream princess newly emerged from the caves of Ajanta and Ellora. And in addition to all this, she should have the breeding of a very good family.

The income would remain the same as it was during Surajmal Kanodiaji's time. In addition she would have a respectable place in society, hobnob with Europeans, and accompany him on a tour of Europe at the end of April. Actually he was cutting back many of these activities since they were affecting his health. As for Surajmal, it was best that he be completely ignored, although he made it very difficult to do so.

Nilofar had firmly decided that she was going to reject Raja sahib, but he didn't give her a chance to reject him. He made no uncouth and impolite demands and he didn't even ask Nilofar whether she agreed to his terms or not. It was as if he had just given her an order.

Rani sahiba had stopped speaking to him a long time ago, but the children were being raised under his supervision. Despite his long estrangement from his wife, he was still impressed by her. He regarded her as a treasure trove of learning and knowledge. He dressed his mistresses the way she dressed her daughters. She was considered ultra modern in society. Her taste and fashion were renowned. The very next day Raja sahib had new clothes made for Nilofar; instead of shimmering Banarasi saris he bought outfits modelled after the Ajanta styles; instead of jewellery crafted with gold and jewels, he bought antique jewellery that was now the rage.

Nilofar became a puppet in Raja sahib's hands. He didn't give her a chance to think and she, on the other hand, didn't feel the need for it. What room was there now for rumination? All of life's secrets had already been revealed to her and she was resigned to whatever her fate would bring. What remained to be seen was which lap she would fall into when she leapt from here. And then a day would come when her leap would become suspended in a void, or she would land on a rock and be shattered to pieces. Why did everyone tire of her so quickly? She thought too much and when she did so, someone or the other would disapprove.

She couldn't understand why Raja sahib had spent ten to twelve thousand rupees on her. For some reason, she was feeling apprehensive. When she asked him in a tone of complete sincerity, he smiled.

"Look my dear, I'm not one of those people who says one thing and does another. I'm not your lover, I'm your friend. Why should I hesitate to spend money on things which make you happy and which don't result in a loss for me?"

"The wretch is lying, and showing off," Nilofar thought. "He's trying to impress me." But if he hadn't spent ten thousand rupees she would still have got out of the manager's clutches. There must be some mystery in all this, she thought, but remained silent.

"I don't believe in making money by not paying taxes or by bribing someone. I have to mingle with members of high society. You don't have to do anything except travel with me because I hate travelling alone."

"And Rani sahiba?"

"I'm talking about business, not recreation. I don't have a single moment to waste."

"But I should know exactly what I'll have to do."

"Nothing. Just act as a hostess."

"But I don't know how to be a hostess."

"Don't worry about that. You're a born hostess. And I'm with you, so don't worry."

"But for this job any well-educated girl ..."

"Look, forget the well-educated girls. All they are good for is becoming teachers. We need good looks as well. Actually, Miss Ahmad stayed with me for many years. The stupid woman would go off every year to get married and three months later she would come back to me, crying. She had started casting her net to catch important officials. I tried to explain that she was wasting her time getting married, that it was not in her blood, and also, that she was discrediting me."

"But how could she discredit you?"

"Oh, you don't know anything. I have to maintain a proper relationship with the wives of these officials. Under these circumstances they become my enemies. There's no harm in having friendships, but she would take it into her head that she had to get married. This would lead to all kinds of problems. I'm warning you as well. I've heard that you had wanted to marry Seth Surajmal Kanodia."

Embarrassed, Nilofar lowered her head and said nothing.

"Actually, I don't want to say this, but the truth is ..." He stopped in mid-sentence.

"No, no, please go ahead. Why stand on ceremony."

"I wonder why women are so fond of the idea of marriage. I have known very liberal-minded women and in the end they all stop at marriage. One shouldn't mix business with marriage. Will you wear that nylon gown?" He changed the subject suddenly.

Nilofar was astounded.

Raja sahib didn't turn out to be as business-minded as he professed to be. His way of expressing love was strange indeed. One day he got drunk and broke into sobs.

"I'm very unlucky. People misunderstand me. No one has ever tried to look into the depths of my heart. People think I'm an alcoholic, that I'm debauched. But I'm in my senses. Aren't I in my senses?" he asked her between sobs.

Then, weeping, he told her the story of his first love. How he had fallen madly in love with a Parsi beauty, but the selfish members of his state separated him from her.

"I'm very unhappy. I need love. I need true and unselfish love. If a woman wishes it, the desire to exist can be rekindled in my heart. Masooma bibi, love me."

From somewhere far away, someone said, "Masooma

bibi, wrap your dupatta about you carefully, the holy Quran is right in front of you."

Nilofar looked at Masooma and burst into tears.

"Masooma bibi, you're crying. Are you feeling sorry for me?" Raja sahib began sobbing heavily again. All wrapped up in a dupatta, Masooma is pacing back and forth as she recites the twenty-ninth sipara. Next Friday she'll complete the Quran Sharif. Then the *aameen* ceremony will be celebrated. Pink silk pyjamas and pistachio green net dupatta. Swirls of fire began to rise at her back. The flames from the mehndi bushes planted by Dada arose and spread all around her.

"The name you had in school will be fine – Masooma Bano."

"No," Nilofar said irately. Far away, away from her world, her classmates, Farkhanda Anwar Ali, Tehmina Merchant, Gulbano Wazir Hassan, Laura Pearson, Masooma, have all been separated. They're alive, but Masooma has died and she can't drag her from her grave. The white crawling worms have not even left the earth in the grave intact. No, don't disturb her. Otherwise, this dream too will be shattered. Don't crush her virginity.

But Raja sahib stubbornly insisted she take her own name.

"Nilofar sounds like the name of a prostitute. You won't understand this fine point but my position in society will suffer. A name reveals whether a woman is respectable or not. Only the discerning can understand this."

"Understand what?"

"After the police action in Hyderabad, many prostitutes started claiming they were the daughters, daughters-in-law, or relatives of this raja or that official, that their husbands had left for Pakistan and they began to be sold at the same rates as girls from respectable families."

"But what difference does it make?"

"It makes a great deal of difference. A different label is important, despite the fact that what's inside the bottle is the same. Eating the same chaat and pakoras that are sold by the wayside is much more enjoyable in a restaurant."

"All right. Can I ask you something?"

"Ask my love, ask not one but a thousand questions."

"In the business ... I mean, is this enough?"

"I don't understand."

"Are women and parties ..."

"No, my love. Don't say that. They are just like spices. Parties and social gatherings are superficial, just to cook the chicken."

"Chicken?"

"Yes, to cook it, make it tender. You don't know how many fools there are in the world. A couple of parties, first-rate alcohol, beautiful girls, and people open up a bit. Exchanges are facilitated, and finally lead to strong friendships. And once that happens, anything is possible. After a few parties, then, as the saying goes, the chicken is cooked."

"But I've heard that many bribes have to be given."

"Yes, my dear, that's true, but you have to be in a high position even to give bribes, you need a special way of getting there. You can't just go and hand over the money. There's much more involved. How to give, to whom, how much and in what way. There are some who appear reluctant to take the bribe and won't accept it themselves. They'll say, 'Oh, I have a widowed sister, she has daughters to marry, you know, my income is limited.' This is the only hint you need. We send off to his widowed sister yards of fabric, jewellery, cars and anything else he has quietly requested."

"And what about someone who doesn't have a widowed sister?"

"I've never met anyone who doesn't have a widow or an orphan in his family. As a matter of fact, it seems that these days influential people have platoons of orphans in their families. Perhaps their own children are also orphans."

"Aren't these people ever caught?"

"Who will catch them? The only person able to throw the first stone at the adulterer is one who has never committed a sin himself. In any case, we never play a game that is even slightly flawed. And those on the take aren't fools either. Let me just say that I have accounts in all the best hotels in the city. If someone goes there and says, 'I need a room', and gives his name as 'Gulabchand', the manager will give him a room without asking any questions and put the tab in my account. Then when calls are made to a cloth merchant or a jeweller from there, whatever business has been decided on and for an amount fixed beforehand, will be conducted in Gulabchand's name. There will be no bill and no receipt. Now I challenge anyone to catch Gulabchand."

"How extraordinary!" Nilofar's eyes widened in surprise.

"There are other ways of doing this too. Look, if I'm a friend I can give the daughter-in-law a car as a wedding gift. What can anyone do? I'm a raja, not some pauper that I can't give a diamond set as a gift or not be able to lend a hand with the wedding expenses. Have tents and marquees put up, arrange for the lighting, supply cars – there are a thousand ways of going about this. Only someone who is drunk or on drugs will try to nab me."

"But what do you get in return?"

"Whatever I need. For example, a contract, supplies that need to be disposed of, a plot of land. Just recently I had a lot of trouble with a property – a girls' school. I bought the property from the owner. I have plans to build an air-conditioned cinema hall there. We have the approval of the trustees, but the headmistress is creating a ruckus."

"So what will you do now?"

"Well, just wait and see what I'll do. The headmistress is

a Christian and has been running the school for twenty years. Now we're trying to somehow speed up her retirement, which is not really possible."

"Why?"

"Because she can continue working for another ten years. Also, she has the girls on her side. If she had come to me directly and asked for help, I would have relented, but she was behaving so arrogantly that I didn't want to give in. I'll have to go to Bombay and check out some other possibilities."

"You'll have to check whether the chicken is cooked or not."

"Yes." Raja sahib started laughing.

"Have you put in enough garlic and ginger?"

"What?"

"To cook the chicken."

"Oh, yes, don't worry about that. Let's go to Bombay first. We'll have a grand party there. What do you say?" He walloped Nilofar's hip.

"Ohh ..." Nilofar cried coquettishly. And suddenly the weight on her chest disappeared. A thousand laughs bubbled inside her, as if she had just received her exam results and found that she had passed with flying colours. There were those who had fewer points than her and were sitting smugly with impressive degrees pressed under their arms. She was not so unsuccessful after all.

This became a reason for her to drink to her heart's content and, forgetting business, she made love so generously to Raja sahib that the memory of the films she had seen which had nauseated her faded away.

In Raja sahib's company Nilofar saw the world revealed in its many forms. Each form was darker than the one before it. In the stormy sea of sin, she was a mere drop. Everyone was either a little more or a little less powerless than her. They readily and willingly placed shackles around their ankles.

When sin becomes a necessity of life then it's no longer sin, it is a requisite of good judgement. In a public bath where everyone is naked, why should she feel uncomfortable about her own nakedness? In a few months she had augmented her value three or fourfold. Calcutta, Delhi, Bombay, Madras – in short, Raja sahib's parties were very successful in all the big cities.

While Nilofar was in Delhi she received a letter from her mother. She had gone to see a young man for Zubaida who was completing her last year of a BA. Amma had been checking out several young men for her. She had various demands; the value of the donkey is equivalent to what the donkey is worth. The mention of her sister's wedding cut deep into some part of her heart. Masooma hadn't died yet; there was still some life left in her. Was she jealous of her sister? Was she envious of her virtuous, pure existence? Not at all. She had always loved Zubaida. She was awkward and fond of studying. Providing her with an education had proved greatly satisfying; she had made up in this way for some of the deprivations of her own life. She wrote to her mother to look without hesitation for the highest quality goods for Zubaida and not be frugal. She felt very calm after writing the letter. That night she was very lively, and created quite a racket. She was cuddling up against a poet, who was whispering lewd verses in her ears, and Raja sahib was elbowing her repeatedly because he wanted her to pay attention instead to Gauhar Maqsood, a very important personage. She was sick at the sight of Gauhar Maqsood's bald head and soft eel-like face, His eyes and nostrils were red, as if he had been weeping or was about to.

"I say, let Colonel sahib taste a piece of that kebab, and look, his glass is empty. Listen, why don't you tell Colonel sahib that joke you told me the other day, the one about the bathroom that made me bend over with laughter." Again and again Raja sahib tried to rope her in and bring her back into the coop. Colonel sahib was very drunk and all over her, trying desperately to keep her amused. While he was attempting to put an ice cube in her glass, his aim strayed and the ice cube slipped down her front of her kameez. Flustered by Nilofar's screams he hastily put his hand in and the ice cube slipped further down and his hand landed on embers. Nilofar, who was very drunk, couldn't remember what she did next. Everyone at the gathering began to warm their hands in search of the ice cube.

When she awoke the next morning she found herself in a strange room. Next to her on the pillow was a large egg. But it was cracked down the middle, as if the chick was about to hatch. For a long time she wasn't sure if she was in some desolate jungle, but then suddenly it revealed gold-capped teeth.

"Ohh ..." She covered her eyes with her hand.

"Miss Jang, I'm really sorry."

"You deliberately got me so drunk," she said, putting on her act. The poor fellow hadn't done any such thing.

"You ... you ..." he stuttered.

"I want to die."

"Please ... darling."

"Please send for a taxi."

"The car is here, but ..."

"What do you take me for?" She pushed away the hand crawling on her thigh.

"Oh my God. Listen, please." Colonel sahib knew who she was, but admitting her true identity was insulting for him. How satisfying was the thought that he had forced himself upon a cultured girl from an elevated social class.

"I'm a swine," he said proudly.

Nilofar hid her face in the pillow and began to cry. She herself was surprised that her tears gushed involuntarily without her having to poke her eye with a finger. Actually she couldn't stop crying. Why? She was astounded. When Colonel sahib placed his head on her feet, she should have started laughing. But some overwhelming power beyond her control was weeping inside her. When the storm passed and the clouds scattered, she drank some lemonade and realised she was in the Ashoka Hotel.

"My God, what a temper," Colonel sahib said lovingly as he rubbed the bump on his head. He had suffered such great wounds in battle, his uniform was covered in medals, but he had never been blessed with such a beautiful wound, inflicted by such a beautiful beloved before. That was why he was looking at her with such a honeyed gaze, and instead of anger, he appeared grateful. He must have been at least a major during World War II since he was not only bald but the frill of hair on his head was also nearly all grey.

Nilofar felt sad. Why was she destined to receive only such rejected mangoes. Would she never be able to swing from the embrace of strong, young arms? Beginning with Ahmad bhai, all the way to Colonel sahib, every man she had known had been either twice her age or even older. Suddenly she remembered the taxi driver. He must have been young. If only she had not been so drunk!

They were in the middle of breakfast when Raja sahib made an appearance.

"Aadaab arz. And how are you dear sir?" He started teasing Nilofar just like a younger brother-in-law. "You two disappeared from the party and we kept looking for you. The party broke up after you left. You fooled us."

Nilofar stood up and walked out to the balcony and soon Raja sahib and Colonel sahib were deep in conversation. There was some mention of machines. Nilofar remembered that Raja sahib owned a factory where besides locks, some auto spare parts, stoves and tiffin carriers were made. Perhaps he was on the hunt for a substantial contract.

On the lawn below some ayahs were strolling about with children. Seeing a dark-skinned child Nilofar suddenly thought of her daughter. What was her name? She had forgotten. When she was born, Nilofar had wanted to give her a name that would rhyme with the names of the seth's other daughters. Usha Rani. But sethji had looked embarrassed at her request. He wasn't ready to put this child as a link in the chain that contained names like Sheela Rani, Pushpa Rani and Indra Rani. Finally her name was registered as Firoza Bano. As a young man, he had been in love with a girl called Firoza. She had gone to Lahore and might be a high-class madam by now.

Nilofar had been disappointed which is why she always forgot her name. She had felt sorry for this unattractive girl who had forced her stay in her womb for nine months. If it had been a boy perhaps the seth would not have cut her off so hastily. She had allotted the seth a corner of her heart, but ever since it had become vacant it was like a desolate, uninhabited palace. Now she wouldn't hand over even a broken down corner to anyone.

"Actually the local market is practically non-existent, and on top of that the bastards have thrown their nets everywhere."

Raja sahib was explaining the finer points of business to the Colonel. "They have installed small kilns in their houses."

"But how will this affect your factory?"

"It does affect us quite a bit. This cottage industry eats us from the inside like a worm. You have no idea how much labour is lost. The buffing of various parts of the locks is done by us with imported instruments, but this is being performed for them by women who do this part-time after their household chores. Tools are cast in these kilns and given to people who take them away for polishing and the job is accomplished at a very low cost. Just think, how many workers we lose."

"But do you have any dearth of labour?"

"Well, it's not that easy either. Because the women who work from their homes can't go to the factories, and we can't use them. And secondly the owners of small factories keep them under their control. We have been boycotted. All kinds of nonsense is fed to these workers. They'll be made to work for free and won't have any rights, they're told, and then they are tempted to do part-time work only and not work the full day. We can't organise labour. They are provoked by any kind of routine. What can I say? The poison has spread far and wide. Like roadside vendors, they sell locks, stoves and lanterns from door to door and set up small roadside shops. They've dominated the market. How can we compete with them? It's hopeless, and our shops are nearly deserted all the time. It's obvious that these small shopowners sell goods at lower prices."

"Even if compared to your goods what they sell is rubbish?"

"Of course. People don't have enough brains to appreciate something that is more durable. They will buy the same thing ten times, but it should be inexpensive. It's a strange mindset. And in addition, I resent the sowing of the seeds of hatred that pits one group against another."

"Can these people not be arrested for selling defective goods?" Colonel sahib asked, yawning.

"No sir, we've tried that too. They have been allocated official licences and their goods are not actually defective. Actually, they are technicians who were working in factories before this."

"But this factory has been shut for a long time."

"Yes. I bought it from Nawab sahib. I can't tell you how much capital I have invested. I've put in new machinery, hired trained staff. Colonel sahib, we also have the right to make some profit. First they seized our states and now they want to take possession of our means of livelihood too? Wherever we invest capital, we run into the same difficulties.

The government's laws have shackled our hands and feet. The police assist them. And then they say, 'Capital is hard to come by.' What do we care? If our money stays in our lockers it will remain safe at least. If we invest in the nation's economy, then we will become bankrupt. If there's no decision made, then I'll sell this factory for whatever I can get and migrate to England. I have enough to make ends meet."

"Oh yes, I just remembered. What happened to the yacht you had?"

"I have it. You should come some time, we'll sail on the Jamuna whenever you wish. Listen, if you like it so much then ..."

"No, no, I don't have so much money ..."

"What are you saying? Please don't be so formal with me. In reality I don't really like the colour."

"But the colour is beautiful."

"Well, green is just not lucky for me. By the way, what's your lucky stone?"

"Emerald, and diamonds do well too."

"Emerald! How extraordinary. For many generations emerald has not suited our family. Look, I have a request. If you will agree not to displease me ..."

"No, no. What are you saying ..." Colonel sahib started laughing.

"Colonel sahib, don't think for a minute that I'll add this to the account as well. This has to do with the friendship between us. Actually I'm not greedy, sir. I like serving country and nation. Will we be the only ones to benefit if the country is industrialised? The country's collective wealth will increase. And then, are you and I foreigners? We too should receive enough to survive. A person like you, who has sacrificed his life to serve his country, nurtured it with his blood – does he have no rights? Another person with the same abilities as you would be way up there by now. All the textile workers and dhobis are being elevated to the posts of governor, and they are amassing wealth with both hands. But what did you get? The same standard salary! Sir, does any respectable person today get a salary that's enough to maintain a respectable living?"

Nilofar was shocked. She had observed Raja sahib giving orders but had never seen him flatter anyone like this. He had indeed appeared quite concerned about the factory these last few days and had promised her that he would buy her a diamond set once the profits from the factory started coming in. Some arrangements would have to be made for Zubaida's dowry. The bridegroom would have to be given twenty thousand at least for the horse and clothes. It was not too much money for an educated young man from a good family.

She had thought that Raja sahib would take her back with him.

"I have to run an important errand, come with me when I come back," he said quietly to her while pretending to be taking a look at the balcony.

"My clothes are all wrinkled."

"I have your attaché case in the car downstairs. I'll have the bearer bring it up."

Everything she might need was neatly packed in the case.

A few days ago Nilofar had complained to Raja sahib, "He's very ugly," she had said.

"That's not my fault, my love. I had not picked him for this role. If he gets the job done he'll look like a beautiful woman's offspring to me."

What a twist of fate that the very Masooma who had to become Nilofar for the sake of her livelihood, now changed her apparel and became Masooma. Her occupation didn't change, but at least her name did. She suddenly felt that she had climbed back several steps and if circumstances remained favourable then she might actually even become a virgin again. Her ripped shirt-front would be mended and the shyness that had abandoned her eyes would return. In many parties she had been photographed with some very important people and these photographs had appeared in newspapers. Seeing her name, Masooma Jang, next to theirs in the captions under the pictures created a great respect for this new individual in her heart. There were many women like her who were respectable members of society, and about whom there was a lot of gossip, but that didn't affect their reputation in any way. The tackiness characteristic of middle class society didn't thrive here. People were impressed by a woman who boasted a male friend.

Despite the fact that Colonel sahib had retired, he hadn't severed his relationships and maintained strong connections with important and influential officials. There wasn't an important party where he and others like him wouldn't be present. But he presented himself as anti-establishment and he hoped that if he continued to give lectures and statements against the government in this fashion, his powerful friends outside the government would ensure that he would soon be appointed vice chancellor of a university or the ambassador to some country. He had participated in the last election, but toward the end he had withdrawn his name in favour of a very influential and prominent candidate.

"But you said that a huge amount of money has to be spent during an election," she asked Raja sahib.

"Yes, but he received the money for all his expenses, and also benefited from this. One has to have a few opposing candidates in order to capture votes. Then one makes deals with any one party. For many people this becomes a source of income."

"And these young men you've sent for, are they all here in connection with the election?"

"Yes, in a way."

"Where will all these people stay?"

"Besides my own bungalow, I've made arrangements for two other bungalows. Food will be served in tents. I've made sure we've had the crockery and so on counted."

"Yes. There will be a shortage of glasses."

"I've arranged to have enough."

Nilofar suddenly fell into deep thought.

"What are you thinking?"

"I'm afraid. I hope nothing goes wrong."

"No my dear, nothing will go wrong. I've planned to have the police in place as well."

"Yes, but ..." she didn't continue.

"If you're uncomfortable you can make a trip to Bombay. When is your sister getting married?"

"In December."

"I think you should go. After all there will be arrangements to make."

"No, no, how can I leave at a time like this." After a moment's pause she added, "I was just thinking, can't you do this by negotiating."

"If I could get ghee out of a tin without crooking a finger, then why would I want to be involved in all this trouble?"

"But how stupid these people are. Don't they understand anything? They're being offered jobs in their own factory and they're refusing. Have they gone mad?"

"So shall I book a seat for you?'

"Why? Oh no, no, I was just ..."

"I think it's best that you go."

"Why? Is there any danger of a violent disturbance?"

"No, of course not. But even if there is any kind of disturbance, not a hair on your head will be hurt. I think perhaps I should go too. Munshiji, what do you think? It will be difficult for you, won't it?"

"No sarkar. After all we have been loyal for three generations. Even if you make shoes with my skin and wear them, I won't complain."

"Still, you have a wife and children."

"Sir, I've sent them all to Sitapur. Don't worry at all. Who do they think they are, these people, we'll reduce them to nothing."

"The thought of violence is scary, you know," Nilofar said. "Can't one talk to them and explain?"

"Baiji, we've done that again and again. But they demand jobs for everyone."

"What do you mean?"

"Well, they are demanding that all the technicians who are permanently attached to them and those who work part-time, should be given work. There are old men and women involved as well. They say that their livelihood will be destroyed and where will they go. I say to them, well, are we responsible for the whole world? We've started a factory not an orphanage. How else can this country become industrialised?"

"The leaders don't do anything?" Nilofar said, trying to impress with a superfluous remark.

"Oh my dear, the less said about these leaders the better. They think of other people's problems only after they've filled their own stomachs first; it's like a blind man distributing sweets and giving only to those he knows. The first round of favours is for their own relatives, then for those in their districts, so what is left for us? Nothing. And then they have to show the world that they are taking care of their citizens. Except for us, every bit of trash has the right to exist. So I say, what did you get out of destroying us?"

"What a feat," said Munshiji.

"Yes indeed. Now the government is busy developing schemes to give them loans. In other words, instead of providing grass for the goat, the goat is being cut up and fed to the grass. Munshiji, you go ahead and make arrangements for the tickets."

Nilofar didn't understand anything except that the people who opposed the progress of Raja sahib's factory were also the enemies of country and nation. Raja sahib's enemies were her enemies; they were the enemies of that bejewelled necklace that, after all the work was taken care of and the factory was running, Raja sahib was going to give her. They were enemies of Zubaida because if she didn't find a suitable husband she would be destroyed like Nilofar and her entire family would sink into the chasm of devastation!

"Do all that's necessary." She heard Raja sahib give his staff directions and heaved a sigh of relief.

That meant all that was necessary would be done for Zubaida's wedding. Buffet dinner at the Taj Mahal Hotel, reception at the Stadium; the bridegroom and his family would be taken by surprise.

"Go to Bombay without a worry, sarkar. But those people want the payment by tomorrow, because the banks will be closed the day after."

"All the payments should be made by tomorrow. There shouldn't be any kind of a last minute hitch. This is a difficult situation, the slightest bit of negligence can ruin everything we've accomplished so far."

"Will you go to Bombay, sarkar?"

"Yes. It's not a good idea for me to stay here. Whatever happens should happen in my absence."

"I agree, sarkar. If you were here, no one would have the guts to make trouble." Munshi smiled mischievously.

"We'll get the money from the locker today. In this sort of a situation we shouldn't cash a cheque for a transaction linked to the factory. During an investigation these people bother you about the tiniest detail, although I have made everyone happy. We'll stay at the Taj. If we're at some party and away from there, we'll still get the news."

"Yes sir. 'The rose cutting has blossomed!'" Munshiji smiled.

"And if something goes wrong?"

"'The cuttings have dried up'. Sarkar, if I make even the slightest mistake, you can punish me as you would a thief. Umm ... the ... I ..." Still maintaining his respectful stance, Munshiji put on a worried look.

"Yes, yes, come out with it. Has the money for your household been paid?"

"Yes sir, thanks to your generosity, that was paid. My family will bless you and pray for your success all their lives. It's just that your servant is getting married, if only you could be there for two minutes. My reputation will be enhanced by your presence."

"You know I can't return that soon. I'll give instructions to the jeweller while I'm in Bombay and he'll send you the jewellery set."

"Sarkar, that bejewelled set will look like a brocade patch on a rag among the things we poor folks possess. Actually, even if the wedding is not too grand and we can have a normal affair, that's fine. You see ..."

"You want cash? All right, that too can be arranged."

After Munshiji, blessing him and wishing him well, had left, Raja sahib said, "He's a bastard."

"Who?" Nilofar was startled.

"This nasty Munshiji. He wants cash. Doesn't trust me."

"And you're entrusting him with such an important job. Why don't you throw him out, the pig."

"You don't understand Masooma bibi. For 'important' jobs it's bastards you need. All right, let's have some fun today. Wear that special suit of yours – that magenta one. I'm in a very good mood today."

He spoke in a way that made Nilofar feel like a prostitute. "Ugh! May this end up in hell," she thought. But who and what was she sending to hell? The rose cuttings that were about to be planted, Masooma bibi, or the whole world?

The qawwali programme lasted all night. The elite of the city were attending. High officials, national leaders, poets and writers, swayed to the music as they showed their appreciation. Arrangements had also been made for drinks in the room at the back. An enclosure with bamboo screens had been set up on one side for the ladies who observed purdah. Looking like a newly-bloomed magenta flower, Nilofar was rushing about the house like a hostess. The women were whispering amongst themselves.

"She's Dilli Naubahar's daughter."

"She's a film actress in Bombay."

"No, my dear, she's a girl from a very good family, but she went astray, fell for Raja sahib, and ran away from home."

The ladies would gossip but the moment they saw Nilofar approach they would say: "Dear sister, you're doing so much work and no one to help you. It must be difficult."

Pulling her chiffon dupatta free from her heels, managing her loose elbow-length sleeves, Nilofar would sit among the women for a while, then she would get up again.

"Dear sister, I have to send out more paan to the men's section. I'll be back soon." And then she would go and sit with the men.

The audience was engrossed in the rendering of the Urdu and Farsi qawwalis. Raja sahib was a great connoisseur of poetry and literature. The programme was about to end, Raja sahib was reminding her not to forget.

When Nilofar went to the back to have the soda bottles replenished, her heart stopped for a minute. Behind the lawn some fifty or sixty men who looked like hooligans were getting out of lorries with their baggage. Munshiji was directing them to a small tent, but most of them seemed interested in the qawwali. "Come this way, please. You'll be staying here in this tent." He took them to the tent where the gardener had just arrived with a whole case of soda.

"Who are these people being put up in the tent in the back?" Nilofar asked Raja sahib as she handed him a rolled-up paan.

"They're students. They were returning from a trip to the Taj Mahal. Munshiji thought they should be allowed to stay the night here."

"But they look just like dacoits."

"And what about me? I'm also a dacoit out to rob beauty. I swear, you're blooming today." He roguishly pinched her little finger.

Early in the morning the guests finally dispersed. There were still a few people around when Raja sahib, with Nilofar and one of the servants climbed into the station wagon and drove off to the airport so that it would be established that they had left before anything happened.

Nilofar rested her head against the back of the seat and closed her eyes.

"Look my dear, you're not allowed to sleep." Raja sahib pressed a button and a small bar opened up in the front of the seat.

FIVE

SHE IS CRYING. QUIETLY, SILENTLY, she is crying. Her face is lost in the darkness, and no one can see that she is crying and afraid, because the tears running down her cheeks lack the lustre of the stars that would make them shine in such black, dense darkness. Someone is coming up behind her on tip-toe. An invisible bubble, a soft pile of malodorous putrefaction, unseen, unknown that will envelop her in one leap. She's walking, walking on a desolate road, weeping. The monster's long, sharp teeth are smeared in blood. This is the blood of people who, like Nilofar, have walked down this road alone.

Her china doll is broken. She is sobbing, crying quietly, alone in the darkness. The atmosphere reeks of rotting meat and mottled hide, as if hot smouldering metal has been dipped into newly oozing blood. Shards of shattered glass are crawling from her nails to her heart. Tiny fine scissors are nipping away at her brain as if someone is cutting up a silver ribbon and every particle of that ribbon is piercing the parting in her hair like the edges of a razor. Soon her entire existence will be shattered into tiny fragments. The monster is coming at her. The sound of the crunching of its paws is rumbling like the faraway clouds hidden in the sky. Her steps become heavy. The broken doll pricks her palms. An unknown void grows in front of her like a cloud and begins to clutch at her. She screams with all her might, but the air around her remains silent.

She sees that she is enclosed in a gilded grave. The ebony coffin is slowly squeezing her as it shrinks. Yards and yards of kemkhab and chiffon are being stuffed into her lungs. Sparkling jewels are digging slowly into her flesh like the claws of a scorpion. Rubies are slowly oozing like a wound, and pearls are slowly creeping about like worms on her body.

Her breath is gone. It won't return. This is her last breath.

With a wounded sob, she woke up. Her mouth was dry and her tongue was immobilised and rough like the sole of a shoe. Her body was bathed in sweat. Like a sick bitch, she sat up moaning and groaning.

When she was finally able to focus her eyes, she saw that she was lying on a bed in a very grand room. She was trembling. The pillow next to hers was vacant, but the depression in it made her realise she had not been alone at night. For a while she couldn't remember whose head had left that dip in the pillow. She had completely forgotten who she had been with.

But she saw the clothes strewn around the room and remembered she had left the house in Delhi with Raja sahib. She didn't know how she had arrived in this room. Did Raja sahib bring her or had he offered her to a friend, or maybe, as in Poona, had she been handed over to the driver. Feeling isolated all of a sudden, she started shivering. Then on hearing the sound of running water coming from the bathroom, she was startled and quickly jumped from her bed.

"Oh, you're awake."

She broke into a laugh, as if she had found a key she had lost. This golden key to the beautiful door!

"Why are you laughing?" Raja sahib said, also breaking into a laugh.

"Ohh ..." she clutched her stomach and bent over.

"Come dear, rub my back will you."

While she was rubbing Raja sahib's back she saw his body for the first time. She was always so drunk she had never noticed his drooping shoulders and short legs. When he dressed up he looked completely different, she thought, he didn't look so unattractive.

Just then Raja sahib thought of a prank and pulled her into the tub. They had just started playing around like children when the telephone rang. Raja sahib reached out and picked up the receiver.

"The rose cuttings are growing."

He quietly put the receiver down and very lovingly began rubbing soap on Nilofar's hair. After a fun-filled bath they got dressed and ordered breakfast in their room.

"Get ready and we'll go shopping."

"I'm tired. We'll go in the evening."

"We're going somewhere else in the evening. All right, we can send for the saris and jewellery if you want."

"No, they'll bring the same old designs and fabrics. I also have to buy *kemkhab* for the achkan. Which shop were you referring to?"

But Nilofar realised that he was not really paying attention to what she was saying. Again and again he would light a cigarette, draw a few puffs and then throw it away. She picked up the newspaper on the table just to see if there was an English film showing somewhere, and suddenly he snatched the paper from her hand.

"Come on, now, get ready quickly. It's already eleven."

Nilofar swallowed a Saradon pill and started dressing

apathetically. Perhaps she was feeling depressed because of her dream.

Raja sahib opened the door to the treasure trove for her and she bought as many saris as she wanted to. Dinner sets, cutlery, and a tea set were packed and sent off directly to her mother.

"Oh, sahib, how terrible ..." the shopkeeper suddenly addressed Raja sahib.

"Let me have those two pieces of kemkhab and we'll keep what we like," Raja sahib cut him short.

"What's so terrible?" Nilofar asked.

"Nothing Begum sahiba ... the ... the taxes on Banarasi textiles have been raised again," the shopkeeper said, quickly changing the subject.

Nilofar became so obsessed with a pink sari that she completely ignored Raja sahib and the shopkeeper. She draped the sari over her shoulder and soon became absorbed in looking at herself in the mirror.

"My dear, wear this to the event in the evening," Raja sahib said with a smile.

"Ugh! To hell with that! I won't go to that man's house."

"Why treat the poor fellow so badly. He's called twice already."

"I hate that fellow."

On the way to the jeweller's Raja sahib bought one hundred woollen blankets and large baskets of sweets, biscuits and flowers.

"Why are you buying all this?"

"We have to distribute this at the orphanage," Raja sahib said and then made four or five phone calls.

Oh, so that's why Raja sahib had insisted she wear a simple cotton sari. He himself was wearing a khadi shirt and narrow pyjamas of the same material.

Reporters and photographers were present at the

orphanage. Dressed in neat, clean clothes, the children stood like puppets, their faces mapped with astonishment. Raja sahib had pictures taken while he was distributing sweets to the children and patting their heads. Nilofar posed as she gave out blankets and sweaters. Surrounded by reporters and photographers, she was bombarded with questions:

"Where in Bombay do you do your social work?"

She wanted to say: "On A Road!" But Raja sahib intervened.

"No particular area. She just does general work."

"Why don't you work where other professional women are working?"

Nilofar wanted to laugh out loud.

"But that is where I work," she said boldly.

"Yes, Pavanpul and Faras Road." Raja sahib elbowed her arm and quickly took matters into his own hands.

"How shameful that we have attained freedom, but we still haven't eradicated this shameless profession," she seriously repeated a sentence she had picked up from a newspaper.

Two small children from the orphanage draped garlands around Raja sahib's neck and the administrator read a long speech in his honour in which he threw light on his generosity, his munificence, and his humility. And then he enumerated all his good deeds that had bent humanity's back with their weight. He said to Nilofar:

"We are extremely fortunate that we have been blessed in meeting a devi like you. Only noble ladies like you can make our country and nation great."

Laughter began to tickle her throat. She wanted to say: "You bastard, do your mother and sisters also serve the nation like this?"

Raja sahib appeared to be in a very good mood as they drove out of the orphanage.

"My dear, you really impressed them. It's all because of

this white sari. You look just like a temple dancer. If you weren't always fighting with me I could help you stand in the election."

"Oh no, please, this whole thing has left me feeling very uneasy."

"All this uneasiness will end gradually."

"Shall we skip the Colonel's party tonight?" she asked next morning when they returned to Delhi and she saw Raja sahib looking cheerful.

"No, my dear, he'll get upset. He's a villain, that man."

She picked up the newspaper. Suddenly she shouted, "But you said there wouldn't be any bloodshed." She began shredding the paper with both hands.

"My entire plan went haywire."

"Lies!" Spreading the paper flat on the table, she pounded it with her fists and shouted: "Look at this!"

"All right, don't talk nonsense. Get up and get ready. Wear that same pink sari. It really suits you."

"To hell with the clothes."

"So what are you saying? Would you have been happy if the scoundrels had torched my factory?"

"Which scoundrels?"

"The ones who are my enemies and because of whom my factory is about to close."

"Those wretched two-bit labourers? They didn't have the courage to harm you in any way."

"You're really clever aren't you, my dear? You don't know that they were the message of death for my factory. The parts they manufactured were not only cheaper, they were also of better quality. These are the people who rushed to start the fire. What do you want? Should Munshiji have allowed them to burn the factory down?"

"All right, but then how did those college students become involved?"

"These students are scoundrels to begin with. I heard that a few students had beaten up another college student and when students from the other caste heard the news, they were infuriated. How could they remain silent at the beating of their friends? Well, the newspapers have taken this minor news and made a big ruckus about it."

"And what about the police?"

"Well, they arrived late. By that time the fire had been set, the situation had got out of hand. All this was the result of treachery on the part of these very college students. You don't know this, but these people stoop to hooliganism at the slightest pretext. Their mentality is conducive to violence."

"No, that's not true. People in the bazaar were saying that special hooligans had been brought in and the disturbance had been started deliberately. There were preparations made in advance. Acid bombs and knives were used in the attack."

"You heard some rubbish in the bazaar and now you're nagging me."

"But those men coming out of lorries that night looked like ruffians."

"You think that ten or fifteen ruffians are responsible for this unrest?"

"They were no fewer than fifty. And later there were more lorries."

"All right, maybe fifty then. But the papers are saying that a crowd of no less than five thousand attacked the factory. You can see that these people are determined to make a mountain out of a molehill."

"An ember is enough to ignite a fire."

"Are you suggesting that I've been arranging these riots?"

"If it wasn't you then it was someone else like you. Why would those poor labourers who were endangering your factory be killed if the fight was between college students?

Those whose huts and shops were burnt were the very same people who were opposing you."

For a short while there was a deathly silence in the room. Nilofar felt as if centuries of silence had passed. Then suddenly Raja sahib exploded.

"A small-time prostitute like you standing up to me! Have you found a new lover? The more leeway I give you, the more you take. So many times I have said, all this is beyond your comprehension. This is all due to your friendship with Qadir bhai, he's the one who has been filling your ears, the traitor. If I tell everyone the truth about him he won't know how to save himself. The bastard has been gaining supporters by nurturing them with black market money and now he's resting on his laurels all because of it. You call me intolerant? I turned you, a penniless woman, into a queen."

Storms started raging in Nilofar's head. She was equally hot-tempered.

"I didn't say you were intolerant," she said with forced restraint.

"Then what did you say?"

"I was saying ... that ... I was saying nothing." She burst into tears.

"You've called me a liar, a murderer – what more do you want to say? Go and announce this in the bazaar and I'll see who will listen to you. Who do you think you are? If I decide to do what I want, you won't be able to survive in Bombay. You'll end up rotting on Faras Road. No respectable man will even spit on you. And I'll auction that flat and have you out on the pavement in no time."

Her head bent, Nilofar continued to cry.

Raja sahib was not made of wax, but he was not made of stone either and he started to melt.

"What kind of a friend are you? You've seen with your own eyes that the factory is suffering losses. I have to beg for every drop. If I let things be we'll be bankrupt within two days. There's a line of crocodiles waiting with their jaws wide open. You don't understand these things. How much can one cram into your head? We people have so many problems facing us. And as for business, the Hindu merchant is extending his tent with each passing day. Our estates have been snatched, the government doesn't take any steps to protect us and so we have to make our own arrangements to protect ourselves. All right, let's admit for a minute that I used somewhat harsh methods, but how does that mean that I was responsible for the riots? And all this bloodshed in the other cities – is that also my doing? How have I benefitted from these disturbances? I don't have any businesses there. These people fight each other like dogs. It's the lower classes that always kill and destroy. The respectable classes live peacefully with each other."

Nilofar heard the lecture quietly and then fell on the bed with her head on the pillow.

"Now what's the use of making your eyes puffy by crying?" Raja sahib shook her shoulder.

"May all of them go to hell," Nilofar thought calmly. "According to some, I'm a two-bit prostitute, not a national leader. Who knows who is telling the truth and who is lying. Who kills and who dies. Everything happens according to God's will. He's the greatest judge. He will punish every victim Himself. He'll award respect or bring dishonour to those He wishes. These bejewelled necklaces, Banarasi garments, Zubaida's husband's clothes – if, God forbid, there's some hitch in Zubaida's wedding, will the dead rise up? Will their shops and huts go back to the way they were? Where was humanity when Masooma became Nilofar? Who came to place a protecting hand on her head? Here, it's all about playing to your own tune. Who cares if anyone lives or dies?"

"Come on now, are you getting up or are you going to stay in mourning forever?" said Raja sahib lying down next to her.

"Go away, don't talk to me." For a moment the prostitute gone astray came back to life.

"My dear, look at me."

"Go away. I say something and you bully me so harshly. If I have some doubts in my heart, then who shall I express them to, if not you? Should I go and ask the whole world for answers? Shall I go and ask Qadir bhai, the wretch? He always says such harsh and nasty things when he meets me."

"What harsh and nasty things?"

"He asked why a girl from such a respectable family had become embroiled with such people."

"Then what did you say?"

"I said these people are my family friends, that I've come here to buy a dowry for my sister. He was crestfallen when I mentioned the names of Zubaida's in-laws."

"And then?"

"Then he told me that preparations had been made in advance for the disturbances."

"And you believed him and started harassing me. So did he also tell you that these people tried to set fire to my factory?"

"Qadir bhai said that people were specially called in and the chowkidar's hut was deliberately set on fire."

"And the gate that was broken? That too I did myself? And shattered all the windows? You heard this bastard talk and believed everything he said?"

"Why did they burn the poor chowkidar's hut down?"

"Another hut will be constructed. I've already asked Munshiji to give him shelter in the area in my bungalow where we house students and have his house built quickly. I will keep doing what I can for these poor people. Now get up, get ready. He called again."

"Unh! I don't feel like it."

"My dear, he'll get upset."

"Let him get upset. Your work is done, isn't it?"

"No my dear, I now need the bastard for the actual job. What did you think? There is no shortage of these fellows. What will happen now is that new concerns will be raised, enquiries will take place, reports will be prepared."

"And then?"

"The Colonel is a very influential man. He's a bastard. I had made an arrangement with him, and if I now go back on my word and defy him, he'll become my mortal enemy. He'll join up with Qadir bhai's party and create havoc. His name will be on the committee. My dear friend manages to sneak in everywhere somehow or the other. And so we have to tolerate his arrogance."

"May he die, the wretch!"

"May your wish come true. But once this whole affair is over, I'll teach him a lesson he'll never forget. Actually he's crazy about you, the poor fellow. He's been pestering me for many days. He said I shouldn't take you to the Middle East with me."

"Why?"

"He said he'll die in your absence here."

"He should, the dog. I don't care."

"All right, go and get your hair done. That same beehive style bun, and the long earrings we bought today will look good with that."

"But we got those for Zubaida."

"We'll get another pair for Zubaida."

When Nilofar came out dressed in a magenta-coloured sari, her hair done in the special beehive bun style, long earrings swaying from her ears, and all made up, Raja sahib came up behind her and said, "Close your eyes."

"Why?"

"Just close your eyes."

Nilofar shut her eyes. When she opened them again a

gold, bejewelled necklace was shimmering with sparkling rays on her pale neck. She suddenly felt as if molten steel had been poured over her naked body. Her throat became dry and her hands rose involuntarily to pluck off the necklace. But it seemed there was some invisible magnetic power in the necklace and her hands got stuck to it. Raja sahib caught her by the shoulders and turned her to face him and she became taut like a bow in his arms.

Colonel sahib's party was full of verve and excitement. If you observed closely you could see that most of the men were between the ages of fifty and fifty-five. The women were very young and feisty. Certainly no one's first wife was present; all the women were either Nilofar's age or younger. Since there were fewer women than men, people were having a good time sharing. Nilofar and Raja sahib arrived a little late. They had both had a drink before they had left, but the guests at the party had been drinking since five o'clock.

"Ah, aadaab arz." The minute she left Raja sahib's side, Qadir bhai caught up with her. When she tried to ignore him, he started laughing.

"So my assumption was correct."

"What do you mean?" She stopped.

"You got a scolding?"

"What scolding?"

"Don't try to fool me. I can count the feathers on a flying bird's wings."

"Please don't make me solve riddles." She had become accustomed to speaking to men with a lisp.

"You've been forbidden to talk to me. Now look, there's no point in denying it."

"There's no need to deny anything. There must be a reason why I've been forbidden to talk to you."

"Well, the truth is what Raja sahib is terrified of."

"Oh really?" Nilofar felt her anger rising.

"Yes my dear. Because I know all his inner secrets. He's very unlucky, the poor man."

"And why is that?"

"No woman stays with him. His friends and acquaintances make off with his women. The material is worm-eaten, which is why he tolerates the haughtiness."

"You just can't stand Raja sahib, can you?"

"No, that's not true. He can't do me any harm. I have more influence and money than he does. He's just a small landlord who presumes to call himself a raja, while my family has been running businesses for two hundred years. If anyone is envious, it's him. He's also afraid of me. And with this disturbance he has caused now, he'll have to acknowledge my power to deal with it."

"Why?"

"I have a great deal of influence with the press. I'll shred the bastard into pieces."

"So why are you saying all this to me? Why don't you tell him everything yourself?"

"The reason I'm saying this to you is so you can tell him to sell the cinema he owns in Bareilly to me."

"What will you do with that cinema? Why is it so important for you to have it?"

"Well, I just need it."

When Nilofar sought out Raja sahib during the party and mentioned this to him, he cursed him heavily.

"But what is so special about this cinema?" Nilofar became irritated.

"That area is about to be included within the town planning zone. If one has influential contacts then one could get an excellent price from the government. After he buys it from me at the regular price, he'll receive double the price for it."

"But how does he have so much influence?'

"Well, he has seized a weak spot. He's the leader of his constituency and can start making a commotion. He has to be bribed to remain silent."

"In other words, if he makes a profit, the problems that the members of his constituency have are solved?"

"Well at least he doesn't mention the problems in his meetings. He makes over-elaborate statements to newspapers. He's like a butterfly flitting from this party to that party. And secondly, what you don't know is that we're our own worst enemies. One person's head is squashed under another's shoe. So, tell that son of a pig that he'll have the cinema. He can go and see my workers."

"Don't give it to him."

"No my dear, if he makes some committee come after me and start investigations, I'll be dealing with needless headaches."

"If you haven't done anything wrong then why should you be worried about investigative committees?"

"A woman's brain indeed weighs no more than an ounce. My dear girl, this is the real world. You've seen that even before a wounded bird falls to the ground the vultures begin circling around it, and the minute it falls they attack it. Who knows how many people have grudges. They'll chew us alive if they get the chance. Plus, Qadir bhai's family may have been in the business of buying and selling for several generations, but he hardly has any common sense. He's buying the cinema, but if he does not hold his head between his hands and cry afterwards, you can call me any name you like." Raja sahib broke into a loud laugh.

"What do you mean? I don't understand."

"Don't try to understand. That's best for you. I swear you look like a dancer from Indra's court today."

"Stop this now. Tell me why he will hold his head between his hands?"

"There are certain people who are making other plans. And if these plans go through, the entire design of the town planning will change and when the rascal finds out he'll be moaning and groaning."

"Ah, what fun that will be."

"Yes, he'll be stunned. The wrangling is at its height at the moment and no one has any inkling that the plan is still under consideration and that the whole matter is undecided. I want my arid Koyyan plot to be included in the scheme. It's useless and this way I'll get a good price for it."

"What kind of wrangling is going on?"

"My dear, everyone is anxious to get rid of some land. And whoever has the loudest voice will win. They are all trying really hard."

The party was in full swing. There were people representing every sect and every religion. Standing around in groups of three or four, glasses in hand, people were busy bad-mouthing each other. From business, politics and the philosophy of life to natural and artificial body shapes – an exchange of ideas on every colourful and bland topic was in progress. Colonel sahib's face was beet red, either from excitement or the heat of alcohol. He was continuously circling around Nilofar. Again and again he would come and stand behind her and breathe warm air down her neck. His bulging stomach would make contact with Nilofar before the rest of him and she would impulsively burst out laughing.

Qadir bhai was glued to Miss Bharati Sinha's body giving the impression that their bones were intertwined. Mr Engineer was becoming far too free with Mrs Martin. The guests were by now divided into small groups. The harmony on display was grand indeed. People from different sects and provinces were throwing themselves at each other with so much friendly good humour that one could never guess that somewhere individuals from these very groups were playing Holi with each other's blood and burning down dwellings. If this regional conflict was redirected competently and shrewdly to take on the colour of sectarian discord, then nobody would have sympathy for those involved in the ensuing violence and bloodshed. The labourers who had become a threat to Raja sahib's factory came from both sects. They didn't pay attention to their real enemy, the politicians who exploited them, but with great resolve were doing everything to make their plans successful.

It was late at night. Arrangements had been made for a buffet dinner. Innumerable dishes were being served. A few of the guests were eating, but most were still drinking. Nilofar was in very high spirits. Colonel sahib had just deposited the eighth chicken leg in her plate and was blowing moist air down her neck. On one side a gentleman sat quietly by himself on a chair, the tiniest jolt threatening to splatter his drink. A well-known poet had wet himself while sprawled on the sofa. The women who used to shake their heads in admiration when he recited his poetry were now standing some distance away, their noses screwed up in disgust. The men were very happy. The poet was their spiritual black-faced rival and they hoped that his present behaviour would diminish his worth. The servants lifted him up with great difficulty to put him in a rickshaw and send him home. But he was upset that he hadn't had his turn yet. He had not recited his beautiful poems, but people had had their fill because of his extempore poetic act, and no one paid attention to his protests. The bearers dragged him out by force. He was whimpering as he was taken away because he had not been able to shake hands with Nilofar.

One of the gentlemen was constantly apologising. Even after hearing "It's all right," a thousand times, he still continued to beg forgiveness. A woman had misplaced her purse and handkerchief and people were shifting in their seats to help her find them. Her newest admirer was so upset one would think that it wasn't her purse but the Kohinoor diamond that had been lost. He was furious with the people who were indifferent to her loss. Various guests were doing their best to look for her handkerchief inside her sleeve or in her blouse. She would roll over on the sofa, helpless from the tickling of the various searches. No one seemed to mind that she was behaving in this manner.

Nilofar continued to drink on an empty stomach. Every time she looked at the buffet table, she felt nauseated. When you're drunk sometimes you focus on a single idea until you become obsessed with it. For some strange reason she had taken it into her head that the meat being served at the party was dog meat. She also remembered the story of a group in Kanpur that abducted small children, butchered them and sold their meat as kebabs. Again and again she peered closely at the meat dishes. Once she even saw a tiny finger floating in the gravy. People tried to explain that it was a piece of bone, but she couldn't bring herself to believe anyone. And when Raja sahib jokingly dropped the piece of meat in his mouth and chewed the bone, she held on to her stomach, retched and throwing down her plate, ran to the bathroom. She had been observing human eyes and teeth even in the vegetable dishes. Raja sahib had been warning her repeatedly not to drink so much, but Colonel sahib was making a concerted effort to get her as drunk as possible.

All at once Nilofar felt that she was standing alone on a barren rock, a silence raging all around her. She could hear a deathlike stillness sobbing. If someone had asked her before she was born, she certainly wouldn't have agreed to come into the world. Suddenly she felt great sorrow at her helplessness and clinging to Raja sahib, she broke into tears. He seemed like Abbaji to her and she felt she was not Nilofar, but his young second wife, for whom he had abandoned his family and his home. If only someone would love her like that too. Give up his family for her sake. If only she could hide in the embrace of a man with strong arms. Then these fears would not trouble her.

Why was no one worried about her virginity and her femininity? Wasn't she a woman? Her heart also beat for a million sweet words. If only she would become so dear to someone that when Colonel sahib blew his breath down her neck, he would stop him. She clung to Raja sahib and wept. According to the programme she was Colonel sahib's guest today and so he tried to take care of her, but she wilfully hung on to Raja sahib. Both Raja sahib and Colonel sahib started an argument. And she didn't know who won or who lost, who finally held her and handled her.

"Abbajani, Abbajani, please hold me. Abbajani." Weeping and sobbing she fell into a drowsy stupor.

That night she had that horrible dream again. She was walking alone on that same familiar road. The road was panting like a snake, and at its end was a deep dark void. Her sobs froze in her throat, her tears dried up.

As always she woke up screaming. In the semidarkness of the room, she saw Raja sahib's moon-shaped necklace shimmering on her bosom. She lowered her head and the moon-shaped necklace laughed. The pearls smiled one by one. The heads of the labourers, red and drenched in blood and the skulls of little children laughed loudly on her naked chest. She fell from the bed with a scream and began to pull the necklace off with both hands. Colonel sahib soothed her, clasped her to his breast, but it was as if she was in the grip of a fever. She felt revulsion towards him, but fear had made her helpless. At this time even Colonel sahib's presence was a blessing. She kept wailing and whimpering until dawn.

The bridegroom's sisters-in-law and his sisters rapidly made lists of everything being given to her sister. They were loud in expressing their admiration for the moon-shaped necklace. Nilofar avoided looking at the necklace for fear that she might find it laughing again. She and her mother were all over the place, trying to entertain the guests properly.

At the time of the bride's departure, she embraced her sister and cried so much and so heart-rendingly that even the eyes of her enemies filled with tears. A woman guest whispered to another.

"Zubaida is Nilofar's illegitimate daughter."

During the wedding ceremonies Nilofar did not touch alcohol. When her sister, pure and shiny as a pearl, left with her bridegroom, she didn't even wait for all the guests to leave. She retired to her room and drank so much that she was unconscious until the next evening. Sometimes the sound of sobbing and moans could be heard coming from the room, and then a deathlike stillness would prevail.

"I'm all right Ammijan," she would answer when her mother knocked on the door repeatedly. The Begum was getting upset. People were coming and going and the corpse of the princess was shut up in the room.

On the third day the Begum announced she was in mourning. She finally persuaded her to unbolt the door. She begged Nilofar to see a doctor. Nilofar then disappeared for a week.

People said: "She went to the hospital to have an abortion."

No one knows where she had disappeared to for those few days. When she did return she began to revel in fun and excitement. Her laughter tinkled more merrily than before, and she began using heavy make-up to conceal the dreadful condition of her face. Even from my balcony I could count her artificial eyelashes. Once again there were long cars parked in front of her flat all the time.

Now she has developed a dependence on other kinds of addictions along with alcohol. Ahmed bhai was the one who taught her to drink. The dhatoora cigarettes she picked up from Surajmal. The cocaine injections were a gift from Raja sahib. A charming producer made her taste arsenic. In short, every lover gave her something to support her and reduce a little of life's bitterness.

Ehsaan sahib is still around to scratch old wounds. He is attached to this family like a permanent punishment from God. He is so impoverished that even a fly won't get caught in his trap, let alone a seth. His wife and children are starving in his hometown, so he can't go there any more. He has learnt that the world is so big that if he eats one meal a day at a different person's house, that person will not become poor, and for this reason he's always on the lookout for tablecloths arranged with large quantities of food. To this day if some idiot gets caught in his trap, he will open up the bundle of his plans:

"Rajindar Kumar has no dates available. Dilip can't promise any day before October. He says, 'Ehsaan sahib, after that you can take as many days as you like to shoot the film'. I've arranged for three lakhs in advance. And as soon as Naushad sahib returns from Mahabaleshwar, we'll start recording the songs."

But people have now ceased to be irritated by his jabbering. He can't make anyone laugh or cry. At Nilofar's house, he performs the role of a household manager. Arranging for alcohol and food, making sure there is enough soda and ice, remembering to pay the children's fees on time, taking care of bank business, taking and picking up clothes from the laundry, accompanying the Begum to the cinema, and so on.

Before Zubaida's wedding, Nilofar forgave everyone. She went to Surajmal and begged his forgiveness. He was the one who took care of the lighting at the wedding. She herself took the invitation card to Ahmad bhai's house.

"Bhabi, you must come," she urged his wife.

Whenever Raja sahib is in Bombay he always comes to see her. People say that she has a magic root or Aladdin's lamp; no one leaves her threshold without getting his wish. If she is not available herself, she provides a friend.

Her sister Haleema has neither learning nor beauty. The rates for bridegrooms are ever on the rise. They're not happy even after they are given clothes, a car, and a trip to England. It is Nilofar's fault that Haleema remains unwed. If she had not been an immoral woman a respectable man would have married her sister without asking for anything.

When people mock Saleem by calling him a prostitute's brother, he sheds silent tears. Nilofar's heart is rent and she pacifies him by buying him a motorcycle. Zubaida's husband taunts her about her sister's morally corrupt character and she weeps incessantly. Just recently, on the occasion of Eid, Nilofar placated her incensed brother-in-law by buying him a new car – and only then did he come for a few minutes to offer greetings.

This is A Road. The neighbourhood where decent people live. Here live sadhus and saints, who have won the area from Satta Bazaar to Aqaba with the sheer dint of their effort. Some dealers in faith and the world are elevating buildings that are already very tall to greater heights. They are opening grand restaurants with the help of funds obtained from bribery and swindling. They object strongly to Nilofar's actions and her conduct. And if it hadn't been for her friends, they would have made plans to evict her from this colony inhabited by decent people.

But Surajmalji is a servant of the nation. Every other day he performs the opening ceremony of this orphanage or that ashram for widows where long garlands are draped around his neck and bouquets are placed in his hands. Because he is not an immoral person.

Ahmad bhai delivers speeches about compassion and decency in national institutions. As he distributes prizes in girls' schools he lovingly pats the heads of pretty little girls, perhaps so that he can find out which of them is fit to be turned into Nilofar. Because he is not an immoral person!

Raja sahib is industrialising the country. His factory is making excellent progress. He is taking part in the upcoming election. He'll have a seat in the assembly and will do great things for the public. On all the posters on the walls are long lists of his national services. But nowhere is there any mention of the nameless labourers who disappeared and whose families were left on the streets. And there is also no reference made to Nilofar's moon-shaped necklace. Because Raja sahib is not morally corrupt!

And that world, which turned Masooma to Nilofar, is not morally corrupt! It is only Nilofar who is morally corrupt, the Nilofar who supports her family, who is the mother of their illegitimate children, their saviour – she is the one who is an immoral person!

Masooma – Nilofar! Nilofar – Masooma!

Who, as if crushed between the two stones of a grinding-mill, is not a human being but an insignificant grain of wheat which endured Ahmad bhai, suffered Raja sahib and Surajmal, who made a compromise with a living death, with arsenic and dhatoora, who mixed together all the poison produced by the lives of her family members and gulped it down.

Sometimes when there is a commotion in her flat, she comes out and stands alone on the balcony and with vacant eyes looks beyond the red of the setting sun – somewhere far away in the land of dreams – as if searching for her virginal youth that was plundered, for the henna that dried and spread in the sand, the wedding flute whose melody soured, and the magnificent bridal garments that became a shroud!

My sixteen-year-old living breathing daughter
Is skipping rope with her young friends
I wish I could hide her back in my womb!

ALSO BY ISMAT CHUGHTAI FROM WOMEN UNLIMITED AND SPEAKING TIGER

A VERY STRANGE MAN

(*Ajeeb Aadmi*)

'In this novel, Chughtai—whose reputation as a celebrated and controversial icon of Urdu fiction rivalled Manto's—told the story of the Bombay film world of the '50s. There hadn't been a more dramatic and candid account of the tangled emotional lives of Bollywood before this. There hasn't been another since.'

—Jerry Pinto

'The episode of the sleeping pills was covered up. Dharam's condition was attributed to a case of indigestion. Zarina arrived with bouquets of flowers. Smiling.'

This brilliant translation of Ismat Chughtai's original Urdu novel *Ajeeb Aadmi* is the riveting story of Dharam Dev, the famous actor, director and producer, and his all-consuming and doomed passion for Zarina Jamal, the young dancer from Madras whom he brings to Bombay and transforms into a charismatic actress. He looks on in anguish as his betrayed wife, Mangala, a well-known playback singer, sinks slowly into alcoholism. When Zarina abandons him, he is overwrought and dies of an overdose, friendless and alone.

In an interview, Chughtai described this novel about the Bombay film industry as a story based on the life of a producer-director who killed himself after the dancer he had made into a star left him in the lurch. 'I go into why he commits suicide,' she said, 'why girls run after him and producers like him, and the hell they make for these men and for their wives.'

This irreverent, sharply observed narrative of infatuation and ambition is vintage Chughtai.

'A delightful, bold and no-holds-barred novel that rips off several saris and dhotis as it twirls us around the cinema industry of the 1940s and '50s...This novel is a gem.'

—Kishwar Desai, *The Indian Express*

ISBN: 978-93-88070-79-9

www.speakingtigerbooks.com www.womenunlimited.net